Because of Love

Troy E. Moore

ISBN 978-0-578-29692-0

Published by Daddy Bear Publishing Company

daddybearpublishing@gmail.com

For my Lord and Savior Jesus Christ,
through Him, all things are made possible

Introduction

This book initially began as a short story I wanted to feature in a compilation. I told myself I would never write a love story, but I was influenced by the Most High. For God is love. As I grow closer to Christ, so does my writing style. My belief in Jesus will forever be prevalent in my writings. I believe this book is special because of all the trials and tribulations I faced while writing it.

I hope this story will serve as inspiration as well as entertainment. It's not your typical love story. It's not a steamy romance novel. It's a story about everlasting love from a faith-based perspective. I thank God for the privilege of creating the most extraordinary characters I've ever written. I have truly enjoyed writing this book. I hope you will enjoy reading it.

-Troy Moore

Contents

Chapter 1

"Where is your God to save you? Why doesn't He ascend from the heavens to protect you? Your prayers are falling on deaf ears. So just stop it girl, you're only embarrassing yourself."

Three days before

"If our lives were a movie, how would it begin...Honey, are you awake?"

"Huh?"

"Are you awake?"

"I am now."

"Did you hear my question?"

"No."

"I said if our lives were a movie, how would it begin?"

"You know it's hard for me to understand you with that exotic accent."

"You love my accent."

"Yeah, I especially love hearing you speak Russian."

She blushes.

"To answer your question, if this were a movie it would begin exactly like it did this morning. It was a peaceful Saturday morning. The young married couple lay in bed. The husband, Jedrek tried to get some sleep before going to work. While his beautiful wife, Raisa asked him silly questions."

"Ha-ha."

Jedrek laughs.

"Where's the intrigue? Where's the romance?"

"Oh, you want romance? Jedrek grabbed the beautiful Raisa and whispered in her ear."

Jedrek licks Raisa's cheek.

"Why would you do that?" She asks wiping her cheek.

"You like when I do that."

"No, I don't. I'll show you romance, come closer."

"Why, so you can retaliate for me licking your face?"

"I promise I won't. Come here."

Jedrek rolls over. Raisa touches the scar on the left side of his face.

"Why would someone mar such beauty?" She asks.

He places his hand on top of hers.

"The man that did this, he got his."

"Did you kick his butt?"

"Something like that."

"You're a strong man. I'm glad you can take care of yourself."

"You find that sexy?"

"No, I think it's sexy when a man walks away from a fight."

"Some women like to see their men in action."

"I'm not like some women."

"Now that's for sure."

"I don't ever want to see you fight. It would probably make me cry if I had to watch you fight."

"Even if I were winning?"

"Especially if you were winning."

"Some fights you can't avoid."

"I understand that. But some people are without honor. They use weapons to fight their battles for them. I would not want you to get hurt. I want you to be safe. I need you by my side. Promise me you will do everything you can to avoid trouble."

"I promise, but I don't know if I'll be able to keep that promise if another man disrespects you," he says kissing her hand.

"I can take care of myself. I'm strong just like you."

"Oh yeah?"

"Yes."

Jedrek pokes her in the side.

"Stop," she says.

He rolls on top of Raisa pinning her arms to the bed.

"Let's see how strong you are. I've got you, now what are you gonna do?"

Raisa wedges her knee in between Jedrek's legs.

"Really?"

"Yes," she says with a laugh.

"You're gonna kick me in my nuts?"

"Yes."

"That's not fair."

"Fair? You outweigh me by 45 kilograms."

"Don't kick me.

"Then get off me."

"No."

Jedrek leans in for a kiss and Raisa playfully snaps her teeth at him.

"Why do you always do that?" He asks.

"Why do you always fall for it?"

"You've been doing that mess since our wedding day. The minister says, 'you may now kiss the bride.' I lean forward in front of all those people and my wife snaps her jaws at me like she's gonna bite my tongue off."

"I thought you were attacking me. A girl has a right to defend herself."

"You got jokes."

They both laugh.

"Can you get off me, please? I must get ready for work," she says.

"All right, Jedrek says loosening his grip."

Raisa rolls on top of him.

"You give up too easily. You're supposed to be the big strong man and the woman must take what she wants," she says stroking his mocha-toned abs.

"Maybe I like a take-charge kinda woman."

"Mmm...then let me tap that."

"What?" Jedrek asks with a laugh.

"Did I not say it right? I want to tap that?"

"Yeah, I just never heard you say that before. You're so random. I love that about you."

They kiss with such passion. Raisa nibbles and pulls on Jedrek's bottom lip. Jedrek touches her cheeks.

Censored

Chapter 2

Raisa joined Jedrek in the shower as she often does. She claims it's because he hogs the warm water. Jedrek assumes she can't keep her hands off him for one minute. The young couple got ready for their weekend shifts. Raisa prepared a nice breakfast consisting of, pancakes, sausage, and eggs. They left the house at a quarter to 10. It's a short commute to "Rada's Bistro," the restaurant where Raisa works.

"Jeed...Jeed!" Raisa exclaims.

"Huh?"

Jedrek is distracted by the music booming through the car stereo. Raisa taps the volume button muting the sound.

"Hey, I was listening to that."

"You know I don't like music."

"You don't seem to mind gospel music."

"Who could get upset about songs lifted in praise to God?"

"You got me there."

She smiles.

"You do know my name is Jedrek and not Jeedrek?

"I know."

"And my nickname is Jed and not Jeed?"

"I know."

"Then why do you insist on calling me Jeed?"

"It's your nickname."

"It's not my nickname. You're just mispronouncing my nickname."

"It's my nickname for you."

"How can you rename a nickname?"

"I give everyone I care about a nickname."

"Did you give Rada a nickname?"

"I call her boss," she laughs.

"She is your boss."

"I didn't give her a nickname."

"Why not? You've known her longer than you've known me."

"Rada is a good friend, but she's not family."

"What's the difference?"

"A friend can be disappointing at times, but family is always there when you need them the most."

"Not all families get along."

"You're always there when I need you, just like when we first met. Do you remember that day?" She smiles.

"I'll never forget that day. Those two men were giving you a hard time."

"They were harassing me, and Rada did nothing to stop them. Then this kind handsome man stood up and made them leave."

"I didn't like the way they were talking to you. And when the guy touched your butt, I couldn't take it anymore. I don't like when guys mistreat women."

"Some of the other girls let guys touch them to get better tips. I don't like that."

"I could tell, that's why I made them leave."

"What did you say to get them to leave without a fight?"

"I told them I was your man, and I didn't like it when people disrespect you."

"That's why you have a nickname and Rada does not. You have been my champion since the day I met you."

"If I'm so great why hasn't my wife left her waitressing job to come work with me at the shop?"

"Rada and I don't always see eye to eye, but she has helped me a lot."

"I know she's helped you and you feel like you owe her."

"I do owe her."

"The small business loan I borrowed only covered the purchase of the shop and half of the renovations. You gave me your savings to finish the project. You helped me start the business; half of everything is yours. You don't need to work so hard anymore."

"If it wasn't for Rada, I would have never had a chance to save the money. She gave me a job and free room and board. So, I do owe her."

"Yeah, but when does the debt end?"

"When she hires more help, I will hand in my resignation."

"You promise?"

"I promise."

"Getting back to the day we met. I still can't believe you asked me out. I knew you were from another country because women around here don't usually ask a guy out."

"I wanted to thank you for helping me."

"You've been thanking me ever since."

"Lame."

They both laugh. Jedrek parks the car along the curb in front of Rada's Bistro.

"Well, we're here," Jedrek says with a smile.

"My shift ends at six, please don't be late."

"If you go and get your driver's license, we can get you a car, so you won't have to rely on me."

"Are you getting tired of carpooling with me Jeed?" She asks with sadness in her voice.

"No, it's not that. I just don't like the idea of you having to wait on me all the time."

"I prefer to ride with you."

"I don't have a problem with that if that's the way you want it."

"It is…now I shall see you later my lyubov."

"Lube off? Is that another nickname?"

"Lyubov means love in Russian. You're my lyubov."

"Have a good day my lube off," he says kissing her hand.

"Lyubov."

"That's what I said."

She shakes her head at him.

"And don't give me the finger when you get out the car."

"I thought that is how people wave here in America."

"I'm not falling for that. You're joking with me."

"What do you mean?"

"You know people don't wave with one finger. And I'm sure you're aware the middle finger is a lewd hand gesture. Which is why you always give me the ring finger because you don't curse."

"Lewd? Look at you, using proper words now."

"Funny."

"For your information Sherlock, we don't have the middle finger in Russia."

"Wait, so nobody in Russia has a middle finger?"

They both laugh.

"You know what I meant smarty pants."

"I think I do."

"Well, I must go, or I'll be late. Don't forget 'Selfie Saturday'."

"I'ma have to postpone 'Selfie Saturday' until after I get a haircut."

"You should let it grow out," she says rubbing his thick wavy hair.

"Oh no, I'ma keep it cut close. It looks more professional."

"Well, you can trim your hair but leave the beard. The beard is mine."

"Ok, I'll leave the beard. Are there any other instructions captain?"

"At ease soldier. Drive safely," she leans in and kisses him.

She gets out of the car, turns, and lifts her ring finger at him. He laughs and shakes his head. He waits until she enters the bistro before he drives away.

Chapter 3

Jedrek went to "Shady Grady's Barbershop" to get his hair cut. His grandmother used to take him there when he was a little boy. It's located on the other side of the tracks. The place is known to most as the Black Gate Community. It houses one of the toughest street gangs in Tea Town, the Black Gate Boys. This is where Jedrek grew up. This is where Jedrek's mother was murdered. Although Jedrek never told Raisa much about his past. The past still haunts him.

"All done Jed," the barber says brushing hair off Jedrek's shoulder.

"Thank you, Mr. Grady. "Once again you hooked me up in record-setting time," Jedrek says.

"Just showing my appreciation for your business. I know there are a lotta barbershops on the other side of town. You have my respect for coming to the slums to get your hair cut. That shows character," Mr. Grady says.

"It's foolish if you ask me," another man says.

"Shut up! Nobody asked you," Mr. Grady says.

Jedrek laughs.

"I'm proud of you Jed. I know your mom and grandma would be also," Mr. Grady adds.

"I appreciate that. Eight dollars, right?" Jedrek asks reaching into his pocket.

"Put your money away, Jed. I still owe you for the work you did on my car."

"You know I can't let you do that. If you give me a free haircut everybody will start asking for one. You must charge me like you do everyone else," Jedrek says handing Mr. Grady a ten-dollar bill.

"Like I said character," Mr. Grady says pointing at Jedrek.

"You don't owe me anything," Jedrek whispers.

"Thanks, Jed."

"I've always admired you, Mr. Grady."

Jedrek looks at two little boys arguing over a dustpan and broom.

"You gave these boys a job to keep them out the streets. I'm proud of you Mr. Grady for always taking care of home," Jedrek says.

"Get the hell outta here Jed before you make me cry," Mr. Grady says with a chuckle.

Jedrek laughs.

"Yes sir. Y'all have a good one," he says walking out of the barbershop.

"All right Jed!"

"Later!"

Jedrek pulls his phone out of his pocket to take a selfie. Raisa and Jedrek always take selfies when they are apart from one another. It's a tradition they started when they began dating. Jedrek snaps a photo while leaning on his car.

"I think she'll like that one."

He sends the pic to Raisa. Then he tucks the phone back into his pocket and reaches for the door handle.

"Don't move or I'll blow your head off!" A man says pointing a gun at the back of Jedrek's head.

Jedrek lets out a deep breath.

"Who are you supposed to be?" The man asks nudging Jedrek's head with the barrel of the gun.

"Look man, I don't want any trouble," Jedrek responds.

"Well, you got trouble, you come around this neighborhood. Now, who are you supposed to be? Are you a cop? Or are you new competition?"

"Man, I'm not a cop and I ain't competing with you over nothing. So just let me go."

"Nah, I can't just do that. You're in Black Gate territory and I don't recognize you. You're not from around here, so you don't know how things go. But I'm just gonna let you know right now. We don't take kindly to outsiders around here."

"Look man I just promised my wife this morning that I'd stay outta trouble. That I'd try to avoid a fight by any means. So please take that gun away from my head. Before I have to break that promise."

The man laughs.

"You ain't in a position to make threats. I tell you what, I'ma let you off with a warning. Don't ever let me catch you around here again. You feel me?"

"Fair enough."

"The warning was free but a pass to get outta here is gonna cost you. That's a nice ring you got, let me get that."

"Not happening."

"I'ma give you to the count of three to give it up. One..."

"Two, three," Jedrek turns around.

"Oh, you a big man huh?"

"And what, you're supposed to be a tough guy? You're nothing without that gun."

"You calling me out? I could kill you with my bare hands. Trust me I'd be doing you a favor by putting a bullet in your head."

"Put the gun down and put those words into action."

"I like you, it's a shame I gotta kill you. In case you're wondering Burn's the name, 'cause I light turkeys up."

"That's not why we call you Burn. We call you Burn because you caught an STD from that little Chinese woman on Mayfair," another man says.

"Ra, you always got jokes," Burn says.

"Burn, what did I tell you about shooting people in broad daylight?" The man asks.

"You told me not to," Burn responds.

"And did you follow that advice?" the man asks.

"Nope," Burn says.

"Put the gun away and let this man go about his business," the man says.

"Saved by the bell," Burn says tucking his gun into his pants.

"I must apologize for my friend's rudeness… Oho if it ain't my main man Jed. It's been a minute," the man says with a smile.

"How's it going, Rafiq?" Jedrek asks hugging him.

"You must've been gone from the hood too long. You know everybody calls me Ra. Why you ain't tell me you were back around the way?"

"I'm not. I'm just here to get my hair cut. Nobody cuts hair like old Grady."

"Burn you remember Jed, don't you?" Rafiq asks.

Burn shakes his head no.

"Come on man, he used to roll with me before I joined the team," Rafiq explains.

"Did you used to have dreadlocks?" Burn asks Jedrek.

"Yeah," Jedrek answers.

"Ok! Yeah, I do remember you. Man, I'm sorry about the misunderstanding. If you had told me who you were when I asked you, we could've avoided all that," Burn says.

"Burn let me holla at Jed for a second."

"All right I'ma go check in with Rell and Hype," Burn says.

"Keep an eye on those dudes, I don't trust them," Rafiq says.

"Ra, you don't trust anybody," Burn says walking across the street.

"You gotta excuse Burn, he's my most loyal soldier but he's not too big on manners. And I'll make sure a mistake like this never happens again. We look out for our own around here."

"I'm not affiliated with your gang," Jedrek says.

"Of course, you're not, just consider it a favor."

"And the cost for such generosity?"

"No strings attached brother. You're now free to move about the country."

They both laugh.

"So where are you off to, dressed all sharp?" Rafiq asks grabbing at Jedrek's lapel.

"On my way to work."

"Where do you work, the bank?"

Jedrek laughs.

"Do you remember Lester's old shop?"

"Yeah, I see someone remodeled the place. You work there now?"

"I own it. My wife and I bought it."

"Wife? Look at you, new clothes, new career, new woman. I'm glad to see you're doing all right for yourself."

"Thanks."

"Do you have a business card or something?"

Jedrek hands Rafiq a card.

"I'll bring some more clientele your way."

"No Black Gate Boys. I don't want those thugs hanging around my shop scaring my customers."

"Be careful what you say. If anyone of those thugs across the street hears you talking like that. I might not be able to stop what happens after."

"I'm not the enemy"

"I didn't mean it as a threat. Just exercise some caution when you're around here… It's good to see you though. I'ma come by the shop and get my oil changed. Just me, I promise."

"All right Ra, I'll hook you up."

"Bet!"

They bump fists and go their separate ways.

Chapter 4

On his way to work, Jedrek pondered on his encounter with Rafiq. It left him with anxiety and a feeling of guilt. What would his wife think if she knew he had ties to a notorious gang leader? There are things Jedrek never wanted to tell Raisa about his past. Troubling things that might break her heart. He wondered was God trying to tell him something. Maybe it was time for a confession. Perhaps their love is strong enough to conquer any obstacle. Jedrek knows there may come a time when he must tell her. God forbid if she should find out from someone else, it would truly hurt more.

"I pray for the strength and courage to do what needs to be done," Jedrek says.

He pulls into the shop's parking lot. He searches for a place to park in the full lot.

"This day is looking better already," he adds.

Jedrek prefers to walk in through the main entrance. He loves to greet his customers each morning with a friendly smile.

"Good morning, everyone," he says walking through the lobby.

"Good morning," the customers return in kind.

Jedrek sees three of his employees taking a break in the lounge.

"Good morning, guys," he greets them.

No one responds. Jedrek goes to his office and puts his bag down. He looks at his phone expecting a text from Raisa.

"She must be really busy if she hadn't sent a selfie yet."

He skims through his phone looking at old text messages. Jedrek hears the raucous laughter of his employees in the next room.

"We were in the bed kissing and touching. Just when I was about to give her this ding-a-ling, her husband burst through the door," a man says.

The other men laugh.

"Her husband tried to get at me, but she got between us. She was like, 'baby please let me explain.' He wasn't trying to hear that crap. He pushed her out the way. I scooped up my clothes and knocked him down when I ran out the house. I didn't even have a chance to put my pants on. My ding-a-ling was just swinging in the wind. I jumped in my car buck naked and sped off. He jumped in his squad car and followed me," the man continues.

"Squad car?" Another man asks.

"Yeah, her husband's a police officer. He was down behind me, lights flashing and sirens blaring. I was ducking and dodging him at every twist and turn," the man says.

"Did he catch you?" The other man asks.

"Catch me? With my engine? Man, I left his ass in the dust," the man says.

They all laugh.

"Darrell!" Jedrek says.

"What?" Darrell asks.

"Language," Jedrek responds.

"I'm speaking English."

Darrell and the other men laugh.

"Watch your language around the customers."

"Why?" Another man asks Jedrek.

"This is a family-friendly business. No profanity or foul language near the lobby," Jedrek explains.

"Now, here you go again with all these changes. When Lester owned the shop, we didn't have all these rules," Darrell says.

"Yeah, and Lester went bankrupt too, probably because he didn't have many customers, probably because y'all didn't know how to treat the customers," Jedrek says.

"Nah, Lester went bankrupt because he wouldn't stop tricking," Darrell says.

The other men laugh.

"When y'all are in the garage, y'all can talk all the trash you want," Jedrek says.

"You need to chill with all the changes," another man says.

"I tell you what, anyone that doesn't like my rules is free to leave," Jedrek says.

"You can't afford to lose any more people. You just lost two guys the week before last," Darrell says.

"Those guys that came to work smelling like liquor and weed. That did absolutely nothing except sit around talking about liquor and weed. I didn't lose much by letting them go," Jedrek says.

"All right, break time's over. The others need help in the garage. So, let's get back to work," a man says entering the room.

"You heard your supervisor," Jedrek says.

The men give Jedrek dirty looks before going back to the garage.

"Good timing Gus. A second later and I don't know how that argument would've ended. Every day it's something with those guys. I'd hate to let them go but I'm tired of them provoking me," Jedrek says.

"They don't speak for everybody. Most of us are glad you took over the shop. Business is booming," Gus says.

"I'm glad y'all stayed on, it made the transition smooth."

"Darrell's immature but he's a good worker. I'll talk with him. If I can get him to listen the others will follow suit."

"I appreciate that, and thanks for opening up the shop for me this morning."

"No problem, I appreciate the extra hours."

"If business keeps booming, I'll consider expanding. Of course, I'd need a good manager to oversee this place."

"I'm not management material. I'm just a mechanic."

"Don't sell yourself short. You've proven yourself to be a good supervisor."

"Managers are usually the first to get fired."

"Not at my shop. If they pull their own weight. When it comes to pass, just consider it."

"All right."

"I'm going to my office. I brought some changing clothes in case someone needs me to relieve them."

"You're not a mechanic anymore. Leave the grunt work to us grease monkeys. We got it covered."

"Cool. And give the customers in the lobby a 20% discount, along with our sincerest apologies for the foul language."

"Sure, thing boss man."

Chapter 5

Jedrek went to his office to file some paperwork. His filing was interrupted by the sound of someone dribbling a basketball outside. It is a most welcomed sound. Jedrek had the basketball court built behind the shop, mainly for his customers and their families. His employees are also free to use the court during their scheduled break time. Jedrek looks out the window and sees a little girl with a basketball. The girl appears frustrated. Jedrek steps outside.

"Hey there!" Jedrek says to the little girl.

She pauses like a deer caught in the headlights.

"I'm sorry mister, I didn't mean to…"

"Calm down, you didn't do anything wrong," Jedrek explains.

"I don't want the boss to get mad at me for using the hoop."

Jedrek laughs.

"I don't think he'll be mad."

"Really?" She asks.

"Yeah, the boss loves children."

"Then why does he have that fence?"

"It's not to keep the children out. It's to keep the bad people out."

"Oh."

"And where did you come from?"

"I climbed the fence," she says looking down.

"What's your name, young lady?"

The girl hesitates to answer.

"I'm sorry, where are my manners? My name is Jedrek, what's your name?"

"My name is Tory."

"It's nice to meet you, Tory. Why did you climb the fence?"

"My brother and the other big kids wouldn't let me play with them."

"Well, that's not fair, did they give you a reason?"

"It's because I can't shoot."

"Practice makes perfect."

"Easy for you, you're tall."

"I wasn't always, there were times I didn't get picked."

"What did you do?"

"I thought about giving up, instead I practiced, and I got better. Just like you will."

"I can't even make a shot."

"I can teach you if you want."

Tory smiles and nods her head yes.

"Ok. Let me see how you shoot," Jedrek says.

She grabs the basketball and shoots. The ball hits the bottom of the pole.

"See, I can't do it," she says disappointedly.

"You have a good form."

"Form?"

"The way you hold the ball. But I notice you're not bending your knees when you shoot. I'll show you. May I see the ball?"

Tory passes Jedrek the ball.

"Now watch me closely. You hold the ball just like you did before. But before you release it you bend your knees and jump up like this. That will help you propel the ball farther."

"Propel?"

"Throw."

"Oh."

Jedrek shoots the ball, and it bounces off the rim. He laughs.

"I'm a little rusty," he says.

"Cool! You hit the rim."

Jedrek smiles.

"Just practice like I showed you and you'll be making shots in no time."

"Thank you, Mr. Jedrek."

"You're welcome, Tory."

"You can use this court whenever we're open. Just promise me you'll use the front door from now on. I wouldn't want you to get hurt climbing the fence."

"Yes sir. Will the boss be ok with that?"

"I'm ok with that," he says.

Tory smiles. Jedrek walks back into the shop. He listens to the sound of the ball bouncing off the rim.

"*She's a fast learner,*" he thinks to himself.

"It went in!" Tory shouts.

Jedrek laughs. His phone vibrates. It's a text message from Raisa.

"Hello gorgeous," he says looking at the kissy-face selfie.

Chapter 6

A few blocks away Raisa prepares to send Jedrek another sexy pose, holding her hair up with her left hand.

"Raisa! Whenever you're done taking selfies you have a customer waiting," another server says.

"What table?" Raisa asks.

"Table number 12."

"But that's your station?"

"I know, but he requested you."

"Oh, then I shouldn't keep him waiting," Raisa says with a grin.

"It's my station, so you have to split the tips with me."

"Of course, Adira," Raisa says putting her hand on the girl's shoulder.

Raisa walks to table 12. There a man sits with a menu up close to his face.

"Good day sir, my name is Raisa. I will be your server; may I take your order?"

The man puts the menu on the table.

"I don't know what I want to order. It all looks so good," he says licking his lips.

Raisa is alarmed by the sight of the man.

"What do you recommend Raisa?" The man asks with a broken Russian accent.

She drops her ink pen and notepad as sheer terror grips her.

"What's the matter slut, cat got your tongue? I thought you would have forgotten about old Laska. Did you miss me, baby?"

Raisa begins to breathe heavily.

"I guess you're not going to take my order. Good help is so hard to find. No matter, the only thing I want here isn't on the menu."

Laska stands up abruptly. Raisa steps back.

"I still got it," he says with a smirk.

He paces forward. Raisa runs through the dining hall and then the kitchen.

"I'll be seeing you again real soon," he laughs.

Adira goes to check on Raisa. She searches the restroom. She tries to open the supply closet door and finds it locked.

"Raisa are you in there?" She asks.

Adira knocks on the door.

"Raisa!"

"Yes," she answers with a frightened tone.

"What are you doing in there?"

"Is he gone?"

"Your customer? Yes, he's gone"

"Are you sure?"

"Yes, I'm sure! Come out of there!"

Raisa slowly opens the door.

"Why did you freak out like that?"

"I had a panic attack."

"Well, are you all right now?"

"Yes, I'm ok."

"I have something that will make you feel better. Your customer left you a $20 tip."

Adira pulls the money out from her apron pocket.

"No!" Raisa smacks the money out of Adira's hand.

"What is wrong with you?"

"Nothing, I'm Sorry. You can keep it."

"Really? Spasibo."

Adira puts the money in her pocket.

"You sure you're, ok? Adira asks.

Raisa nods her head yes.

"Did that man say or do something to you?"

Raisa has a vacant stare.

"Do you want me to call Jedrek?"

Raisa shakes her head no.

"I'm fine. I only need a moment."

"You shall have it. I'll cover your station while you collect yourself."

"Spasibo Adira," Raisa says.

Laska flees the restaurant and climbs into a brand-new black Maserati.

"Was she there?" A man in the driver's seat asks.

"Yes, she's there. You should have seen the look on her face when she saw me," Laska says.

"So why do we pause? We should go and take her now before she runs."

"Patience Klavdii, I want her to sweat first. Then when she least expects; she will be mine again."

"Is she worth all this trouble?"

"Don't you understand? She's the one that got away."

Chapter 7

"Hey baby," Jedrek greets Raisa as she walks through the door.

"Hey," she responds.

"What happened? Adira told me you took the bus home."

"You were late. I was tired of waiting."

The truth is Raisa was waiting for Jedrek in front of Rada's Bistro when a black car with tinted windows slowly approached. Out of fear she panicked and fell in line with a group of commuters walking to the bus stop. Hoping the group would deter a would-be attacker.

"I'm sorry, I got stuck in traffic. I tried to call you, but it went straight to voice mail."

"My phone died."

"Is everything ok?"

"I'm fine."

"Come here."

"Not now Jeed; I just want to take a shower and lie down."

"Please, just for a second."

Raisa sits beside Jedrek on the couch and lays her head on his lap. He caresses her thick curly hair. She closes her eyes.

"Now tell me what's bothering you, my love."

"Nothing is bothering me."

"Tough day at work?"

"Yes," she says softly.

"That's why you should come work with your man. I keep trying to tell you."

"I don't want to talk about that right now. I don't want to talk about anything."

"Ok, we don't have to talk. Just relax, and let me massage your back and your shoulders," Jedrek says putting his hand up Raisa's shirt."

"No!" she sits up.

"Did I do something wrong?'

"No, I mean not tonight. I want to wake up early for church tomorrow. How about a rain check?"

"Ok…I'll get dinner ready while you take your shower."

"I'm not hungry."

"But I'm making spaghetti; you love my spaghetti. I'm even making those breadsticks you love so much."

"I'm sorry Jeed, I'm just not hungry."

"No problem, we can always save it for tomorrow."

She smiles at him. She walks toward the bedroom.

"Jeed."

"Yeah."

"Maybe just one breadstick?"

He smiles.

"Sure, I'll bring it to you when you get out the shower."

That night Raisa had a nightmare about being chased by Laska. She chose not to wake Jedrek; yet silently cried herself back to sleep.

Chapter 8

Two days ago

Kingdom Israel Baptist Church is a spectacular display. The magnificent structure can seat nearly a thousand people. Far from the original small building Jedrek and his grandmother used to attend. If only his grandmother were alive to see it, he thought. She would marvel at the sight.

"Be strong and of a good courage, fear not, nor be afraid of them: for the Lord thy God, He it is that doth go with thee; He will not fail thee, nor forsake thee," the preacher says.

Jedrek looks at Raisa and touches her hand. She politely smiles at him. The light from the chandelier makes her eyes sparkle.

"The doors of the church are open. Shall there be one?" The preacher asks.

The choir sings.

Whatever you need, God's got it

Whatever you need, God's got it

He's got it, and He's waiting to give it to you

"Amen!" The preacher shouts.

"Amen!" The congregation cheers.

"It's time for altar prayer, please come forward. Casting all your care upon Him; for He careth for you."

Throughout the service, Raisa had an uneasy feeling that she was being watched. Though she tried hard to ignore it. She couldn't shake the feeling. As she and Jedrek walked to the altar something called her attention. She looks up. There standing in the front row of the balcony, Laska. He smiles at her with wicked intent. Raisa looks away. Thinking it but a figment of her imagination, she braves another glance. Laska is still there, kissing at her. She gasps as she begins to step back.

"What's wrong?" Jedrek asks.

She looks at Jedrek. Then she looks to the balcony, but Laska's gone. She bumps into another woman.

"Watch where you're going," the woman says.

"It was an accident," Jedrek explains.

"She scuffed up my new shoes," the woman says looking at her friends.

"Are you all, right?" Jedrek asks Raisa.

She does not reply.

"Let's go."

Jedrek takes her hand and leads her to the exit. The group of women follows them outside.

"Yo Jedrek! You owe me some money for these shoes. They cost more than your little mail-order bride," a woman says.

The other women laugh.

"I'm not paying for those cheap knockoffs, Jedrek says."

"Maybe I'll just take it outta your wife's ass then," the woman says.

"We're on church ground Gina; didn't you hear anything the preacher said?"

"Jeed, you know these women?" Raisa asks.

"Yeah skank, he knows us," Gina says.

"Whoa, watch what you say about my wife. Don't ever disrespect my queen."

"Disrespect? You come here flaunting this little piece of Eurotrash around my girl; trying to make her jealous," Gina says pointing at the woman on her right.

Jedrek looks at the other woman.

"Mya you know I'm not like that. Gina, you need to stop trying to instigate," he says.

"Forget you, Jed. Brothers like you make me sick. You go and get a little bit of success. Then the first thing you do is go out and get a white woman. Sellout," Gina says.

"Words, spoken by a sister that can't keep a man," Jedrek retorts.

A crackhead across the street laughs. Gina mushes Jedrek in the face. Without blinking, Raisa punches Gina with a right hook. Gina falls to the pavement. Jedrek grabs Raisa and pulls her away. The other women help Gina up as Jedrek and Raisa drive off.

"Who were they?" Raisa asks.

"Before I met you, I used to date Mya," Jedrek explains.

"Was she the one with the purple dress?"

"Yes."

"She's pretty, why did you break up with her?"

"I didn't, she broke up with me."

"Why?"

"It doesn't matter. That's all in the past."

"Why were they upset?"

"I don't know. What were you thinking when you hit Gina?"

"She shouldn't have touched you."

"Didn't you make me promise to avoid trouble?"

She scrunches her face up at him. He chuckles.

"I'm sorry, are you upset with me?" She asks.

"No, not at all."

"I feel bad now. We should go back so I can apologize."

"I don't think that's such a good idea. I think we should wait before we try to squash the beef."

"Beef? What does ground meat have to do with this?"

"Never mind."

Chapter 9

Yesterday

Raisa was up early. Her peaceful slumber was interrupted by nightmares about Laska. In the first nightmare, Laska came back to Rada's Bistro and cornered Raisa in the ladies' restroom. She awoke to find herself trapped in another nightmare with Laska standing over their bed. Raisa wanted to tell Jedrek everything. But she's afraid of what might happen. After all, Laska is a very dangerous man.

"You're up early," Jedrek says rolling over.

"I couldn't sleep," Raisa replies.

"Why didn't you wake me? I would've held you in my arms."

"Hold me now."

"Your wish is my command," he says wrapping his arms around her petite frame.

She rests her head on his chest and listens to the sound of his heartbeat.

"It's where you live. My heart, it beats for you," he says running his fingers through her hair.

"'Tis a wonderful place to be, your heart. I never want to be too far from it," she says looking up at him.

"You'll never have to worry about that."

"Let's stay in bed and cuddle."

"I'd love to, but I have to check the inventory and do a purchase order."

"Can't you get someone else to do it?"

"The only other person I trust is Gus and he requested the afternoon off."

Raisa gives Jedrek a sad look.

"I'm surprised at you. You rarely take a day off," he says.

"I've been thinking about what we discussed before. About my coming to work with you at the shop."

"Yeah."

"I'm ready."

"For real?"

"Yes, is that ok?"

"Hell yeah! I'm sorry, I mean yes. When do you wanna start?"

"Immediately."

"What about Rada? Aren't you gonna give her two weeks' notice?"

"I'll call Rada and tell her I resign. I don't ever want to go back to the bistro."

"Has it gotten that bad there?"

"You have no idea."

"Did something happen between you and Rada?"

"No, I'm just ready to move forward."

"I like the sound of that. This calls for a celebration. Do you wanna go out tonight?'

"No, I'd rather stay in."

"Ok, well I'll stop and pick something up on my way home."

"There's one more thing."

"What's that?"

"Do you think maybe we could take a trip?"

"You wanna go on vacation?"

"Before I start."

"Ok, where would you like to go?"

"The islands."

"I think we can take some time off."

She smiles in delight.

"We should go and never come back," she says softly.

"As nice as that sounds, you know we can't do that. All our money is tied into the shop."

"I know."

"I'm gonna go and get ready for work," he says motioning to the bathroom.

She grabs his hand.

"Stay with me, please."

"I'm only going to work. You can come with me if you want to."

"No, I'll just stay here."

"Are you ok? You seem very emotional lately."

"I'm fine."

"Well don't sound so sad. You just gave me the best news of the day."

"I'm not sad. I just have a lot on my mind right now."

"I understand. You've been with Rada for a while. I guess leaving there is kinda bittersweet."

"I suppose."

He puts his arms around her shoulders.

"I tell you what, I'll come home as soon as I finish the purchase order. I'll get somebody else to close the shop tonight."

She smiles and nods her head.

"Promise me you'll come home," she says.

"I promise. Is there something going on with you that I should know about?"

"I love you is all."

"I love you more Mrs. Mann. You've made me the happiest man in the world."

They kiss.

Chapter 10

While Jedrek sat in his office calculating the cost of his order. He recalled the conversation he had with Raisa earlier. How different she was. She wasn't her usual playful self. She seemed unhappy. Jedrek knew there was something bothering Raisa but what could it be?

"It's not like her not to call or text," he thinks.

Now he was really worried about her. He grabs his phone to call and check on her. A knock on the door catches his attention.

"Come in," he says putting the phone down.

"Hey, Jed."

"Mya?"

"I come in peace. Can we talk?"

"Sure, have a seat."

"Let me begin by apologizing for what happened yesterday."

"Apology accepted. How's Gina?"

"Her ego was bruised along with her face, but she's fine."

"Do you mind telling me what that was all about, or do I have to guess?"

"The other night I was drinking some wine with my girls. I mentioned how I saw you with your wife. I said some things outta jealously I wish I hadn't said. I truly am sorry."

"It's fine."

"No, I should've stopped Gina. But when I saw you two carrying groceries into your home the other day. I was so angry at myself."

"For what?"

"For breaking up with you. When your grandmother died you became so cold and distant. I didn't think you would ever recover. Then when you got in trouble. I didn't know how to be there for you."

"You did what you had to do under those circumstances. I'm not mad at you."

"Yeah, but look at you. You became the man I always knew you could be."

"You breaking up with me was for the best. When I didn't have anyone else, I turned to God. He revealed to me the error in my ways. And I've been diligently seeking Him ever since. Not to mention I would've never met my loving wife."

"Who is this woman that has your nose so wide open?"

"She's a ray of sunshine in a world of shadows."

"Your queen as you referred to her, somehow managed to restore your heart."

"It was God that uplifted my heart. Then He blessed me with a beautiful woman to share it with. She's never seen me in despair, and I haven't told her about my past."

"Well, I hope she never has to see you like that."

"Me too…I owe you an apology for past mistakes."

"You've always been a good guy, Jed."

"But I wasn't always a good boyfriend."

"I know I might be asking too much right now. But do you think it's possible that we can still be friends? We were friends long before we dated. We grew up together. Me, you, and Rafiq; playing in the playground. We have so much history together. We shouldn't let it all end like this."

"You're right. I don't mind being friends."

"I'd like to be friends with your wife too. Tell her if she ever wants her hair or nails done, come see me at the salon."

"She'd probably like that. She feels bad about what happened yesterday. She was hoping we could squash it."

"She sounds like a classy lady. I'm beginning to see why you love her so much. I can tell she loves you too. The way she jumped in to defend your honor.

They both laugh.

Can I ask you a question?" She asks.

"Yeah."

"Are you happy Jed?"

"I feel the beating of Raisa's heart in my own chest."

"Raisa, A pretty name for a pretty girl. I'm happy for you Jed."

"Thanks, Mya."

"I should be going now. It was good seeing you again Jed."

"I'll be seeing you around Mya."

Mya gets up to leave.

"Oh, Gina said your wife has a mean punch."

They both smile.

"Bye Jed."

"Have a Blessed day Mya," Jedrek waves.

Chapter 11

Mya saunters from the office and runs into Rafiq in the hall.

"What's up Mya?" Rafiq asks.

Hey Ra, how are you? She asks.

"I'm good. What were you and Jed back there doing?" Rafiq asks peeking into Jedrek's office.

"Nothing, fool, so get your mind out the gutter."

"Yeah right."

"You need to grow up. Excuse me," she says nudging him aside.

"I can't say I blame him though. That booty is looking nice."

"Boy bye," she says walking away.

"You should say thanks for the compliment."

Jedrek shakes his head and laughs.

"What's up Jed?" Rafiq greets Jedrek with a fist bump.

"You need to leave Mya alone before she beats you up like in the 2nd grade."

"I let her win that fight. You know I don't hit girls."

"You were trying that day, and she still beat you."

They both laugh.

"What was Mya doing here anyway? Did you hit that?"

"No man, you know I'm married."

"So, what."

"I would never cheat on my wife."

"Is this her?" He asks glancing at a picture on Jedrek's desk.

"That's my queen."

"She's fine. I remember we used to look at chicks like this on tv. And you went out and got one. Does she have a sister?"

"She's one of a kind."

"Man, you lucky. Where's she from?"

"Russia."

"Come on man, not a Russian girl. Those foreign girls are crazy."

"Not mine. She's a sweetheart."

"You must have her tamed. You probably wear her ass out, don't you?"

"I don't discuss my love life with no one. What happens between me, and my wife stays between me and my wife."

"My bad. I didn't mean to offend you."

"It's all right."

"Nice set up you have here. I especially like the basketball court. One day I'ma have to come and school you like old times."

"I haven't played ball in a long time."

"What, as much as you used to love b-ball. What happened?"

"A knee injury."

"I don't remember you getting hurt on the court…Oh, it happened when you got sent away."

"Yeah."

"I'm sorry that happened to you. I always thought you were good enough to play pro ball."

"You were pretty good yourself."

"Good? All city baby, three-time conference champs. We made a great team, didn't we?"

Jedrek nods his head in agreement.

"Of course, if I hadn't dropped out you wouldn't have gotten any minutes," Rafiq boasts.

"Coach always thought you were better. You just took more shots, ball hog."

"Whatever, I made those shots."

They both laugh.

"Do you ever wonder what could've been?" Rafiq asks.

"Yeah, but God had other plans for me."

"Well look at you all grown up. Sitting in that chair looking like a boss."

"I am a boss."

"It looks good on you bro."

"Thanks. Did my crew take care of you?"

"Yeah, you weren't kidding with that advertisement about speedy service. And I can't argue with those prices either. You need to up your prices or you'll be outta business soon."

"They're just standard prices."

"Yeah, but your competitors are making more money."

"They're making more money, but they probably don't sleep at night. I try to be fair with my prices. I don't wanna be greedy by robbing my customers blind."

"Being fair doesn't keep you fed."

"They get the same discounts on materials as I do. What would I look like if I charge three times the amount?"

"A smart businessman."

Jedrek laughs.

"It's better, to be honest. You can't get away with cheating people. God sees everything. I try not to think about how much more money I could be making. Besides, whatever I need God's got me." Jedrek says.

"God? Whatever man. I tell you what if you wanna start making some real money. I can hook you up."

"What do you mean hook me up?"

"I got a few boys that boost cars. They can bring the cars here. You already have all the tools we need to strip them. I can give you a piece of the action."

"You're not turning my place into a chop shop."

"I don't mean during the day. It would be done at night. You wouldn't even have to be here. Just give me a key to the shop."

"I don't think so. You must be high if you think I'd consider something like that."

"You forget where we're from? We grew up in a neighborhood where if we wanted something bad enough, we took it. Because nobody was ever gonna give us anything."

"You need to let go of that old-school logic."

"It was that same old-school logic that saved your ass not too long ago. Which I often wonder. Where did you hide the gun?"

"Don't worry about that. It's in a place no one will ever think to look."

"I don't like the idea of you having that over me."

Jedrek smiles.

"You'll just have to trust me," Jedrek says.

"I'm supposed to trust you, but you can't trust me enough to do business. You got some nerve."

"I have the nerve? What about you stealing from your own people?"

"I don't steal from our people. I steal from white people; for your information."

"You're still robbing your own. What do you think happens when you steal something from an upscale neighborhood? They raise the price of things in our neighborhood to compensate for the loss in theirs."

"You're getting a little too deep into this. It's not that serious."

"You keep fooling yourself into thinking it's not."

"You think I'm such a crook? What about you, hypocrite? You stole this shop."

"I didn't steal the shop. I bought it fair and square."

"Oh really? I seem to remember Lester being in a lotta debt. You probably bought this place for dirt cheap."

"That's business."

"Business? You talk a good game about helping people but why didn't you help Lester? You were too busy helping yourself. You could've easily loaned him the money to keep his shop. You and Lester could've been partners. Instead, he's out in the cold because you bought him out."

"How do you know I didn't consider partnering with Lester? That I prayed and fasted for an answer. God gave me the discernment that Lester couldn't be trusted."

"So, God told you to cut Lester out?"

Rafiq laughs.

"The only difference between us, is I don't hide behind the law to take what I want," Rafiq says.

"Thank you for stopping by. I appreciate your business, but I think it's time for you to go."

"You kicking me out now? To hell with you Jed. I've always had your back. When no one else gave a damn about you. Now you spit in my face. I hope for your sake you never need my help again. At this point, I wouldn't piss on you if you were on fire."

"I don't need your kinda help."

"In that case, I suggest you stay away from Grady's. Next time I won't stop Burn from putting a bullet in your head."

Rafiq storms out. Jedrek lets out a deep breath.

"I'll continue to pray for you, my brother."

Jedrek grabs the picture on his desk.

"I can't hold it in any longer. It's time I tell her everything."

Jedrek resumes his duties instead of calling Raisa. His plan is to conclude business without further interruptions.

Chapter 12

At home, Raisa toyed with the idea of calling Jedrek, but she chose not to. She believed any distractions would only delay his arrival. Raisa tried to do things to occupy her mind. There were no chores to be done. She decided to read a book. She took a break from reading to surf the web for vacationing spots and rates. She was very tired but too afraid to sleep. A knock on the door startles her. The only person she's expecting is Jedrek and he wouldn't need to knock. She slowly walks to the door.

"Who is it?" Raisa asks.

"My name is Ashley. I'm sorry to bother you miss, but I'm lost. I'd appreciate it if you could give me some directions," a young lady says.

Raisa looks through the peephole and sees a girl standing in front of her door. Raisa opens the door.

"Hello."

"Hey," Ashley says.

"How may I help you?" Raisa asks with a smile.

"I just need some directions."

"Where are you trying to go?"

Ashley looks to her side.

"I'm so sorry."

"Sorry? For what?" Raisa asks.

Laska peers from the blindside.

"No!" Raisa shouts; trying to slam the door.

Laska pushes the door open, forcing his way in, dragging Ashley in behind him. Laska throws Ashley to the floor. Raisa is paralyzed with fear.

"I'm so sorry. He made me do it," Ashley cries.

"Shut up! Say another word and you're dead." Laska says.

Raisa breathes heavily. Laska smiles at her.

"Hello my pretty," he says.

"Get out…Get out of my house before my husband comes home." Raisa shudders.

"Your husband?"

He laughs.

"He will be here any minute."

"Your husband must be a fool to leave such a prize unattended. I've been thinking, he is either a coward or he doesn't know about me…You never told him about me, did you?"

"I couldn't. He would have gone after you."

"I can imagine. The monkey would probably beat me in a fight."

Laska draws a gun from behind his back.

"You did right not to tell him. I would have ended his life before he could raise his fists."

"What do you want from me?

"You caused me a lot of grief."

"Have you come to hurt me?"

"You're getting warmer."

"I ask that you leave my husband alone. He's never wronged you in any way."

"I don't care about that animal you married. If he stays out of my way, he can keep his pathetic life."

"Are you going to kill me?"

"I'm going to break you. Day by day, night by night, piece by piece; until there's nothing left. You'll live knowing you're nothing more than a curly-haired whore; that I own you. There are worse things than death and you're going to experience them all."

"I'm so sorry," Ashley says crouched on the floor.

"Didn't I tell you to shut up? Laska points the gun at Ashley.

Raisa grabs a vase and hits Laska in the head with it.

"Run!" She says helping Ashley to her feet.

They run out the door. Laska staggers behind them.

"Grab them!" Laska commands Klavdii standing at the edge of the street.

Klavdii dashes through the yard.

"This way," Raisa says motioning toward her neighbor's backyard.

"Get the car. We'll head them off," Laska says rubbing his head.

Chapter 13

Raisa led Ashley away down a narrow path. The path was blocked off by picket fences on opposite sides, making it virtually invisible from the road. They ran for several minutes, stopping to take a breather behind a restaurant dumpster. The two had barely spoken a word since fleeing the house. Ashley looks at Raisa with extreme fright. Perhaps worried Raisa will turn on her for playing a part in the setup.

"I'm sorry," Ashley whimpers, breaking the silence.

"It's ok. I don't hold you to blame for what happened."

Ashley lets out a sigh of relief.

"Ashley, is it?"

"Yes."

"We're going to be ok."

"How do you know that?"

"I have faith."

"Those men are gonna kill us."

"I don't think they will."

"Do you have a phone?"

"I left it at the house."

"Where do we go from here?"

"We must find a way to reach my husband. He will know what to do."

"Your husband? We should go to the police."

"He tried to take me in broad daylight. Do you think he is afraid of the police?"

"I'm scared."

"So am I."

The back door to the restaurant swings open. Ashley shrieks and runs. Raisa looks at a busboy holding two large bags of garbage.

"Ashley, wait," Raisa runs behind her.

"Hey Nick, it's two hot homeless chicks back here," The busboy shouts.

Ashley managed to make it to the intersection before Raisa caught up to her.

"Ashley you shouldn't have run off."

"I'm sorry, I panicked."

"Stay close to me as I guide and perhaps, we can make it to safety. We must hide before we're seen. We are sitting ducks if we remain in the open."

"Thank you for not leaving me. I'll do what you say."

Further ahead a black car skids to a halt.

"It's them!" Ashley turns to dash across the street.

"Quick, this way," Raisa grabs her by the arm and pulls her into a shop.

"Well look who it is girls," Gina says.

"I didn't come here for trouble," Raisa explains.

"You came busting in here like you're ready for round two."

"I'm sorry about yesterday."

"Gina, don't make that girl clock you like she did yesterday," another woman says.

The other women laugh.

"Shut up! The sun got in my eyes, and I slipped," Gina says.

"Yeah right, you slipped into her fist," the woman continues.

Mya steps forward.

"That's enough. Your name's Raisa, right?" She asks.

"Yes," Raisa responds.

"Is everything ok?"

"There are some men chasing us."

Mya looks at the door.

"Say no more. Girls, we're gonna run some interference."

"We got you girl; whatever you need," says the woman standing next to the door.

"Yeah, we got your back," Gina says.

"Thank you," Raisa says.

Mya takes Raisa and Ashley to a back room. Laska and Klavdii run into the shop.

"May we help you?" A beautician asks.

Laska looks around.

"I'm looking for two girls that came in here."

"This is a salon; women come and go all the time. You're gonna have to be more specific," Mya says.

The other women laugh.

Klavdii curses the women in Russian. Laska puts his arm across Klavdii's chest preventing him from stepping forward.

"You'll have to excuse my friend," Laska says.

"Are you a police officer or something?" Mya asks.

"Something," he answers.

"He's not a cop. I've never known the Tea Town Police to hire foreigners," says the woman standing next to the door.

"I don't have time to play games. Tell me where they are, he demands."

"Who?" Mya asks.

"The girl with long curly hair. She was with a Latino girl. I saw them come in here."

"I'm sorry, I didn't see anyone like that come in here. Jasmine, you're closer to the door did you see anybody like that come in here?" Mya asks.

"I didn't see anyone, and I've been standing here for a while," Jasmine says.

"Honey, would you like to get your hair done?" A hairdresser asks.

The women laugh.

"Enough of this crap! Tell me where they are now, or I will make this place very miserable." Laska and Klavdii draw their pistols.

"Freeze!" Jasmine shouts.

Laska turns to see Jasmine pointing a shotgun at him.

"My girl Jasmine works as my security guard when she's not too busy policing the streets. You never can be too careful in this city," Mya says.

"I was at the top of my class, especially when it came to target practice. And I won't miss at this range," Jasmine states.

"So, you can walk out the way you came in, or fall where you stand," Mya says.

Laska grits his teeth and puts his gun away; Klavdii follows suit.

"Now get out before I make your day very miserable," Jasmine adds.

Laska and Klavdii slowly back out.

"Tell those two girls I'll catch them later. And as for you all, you should have thought it through before getting involved," Laska says.

Laska trips over a dustpan as he exits. Some of the women laugh. Jasmine keeps her eyes on the men, making sure they leave and don't return. Mya and Gina rush to the back room. The room appears empty.

"The coast is clear ladies, you can come out now," Mya says.

"Mya, look," Gina points at the open back door.

"Oh my God, they left," Mya covers her mouth in shock.

"Why would they do that?"

"I don't think she wanted us to get hurt. She probably feared what they might do to us if she were found here."

"Classy girl."

"What has she gotten herself into?"

"Maybe you should call Jed."

"Let's see what Jasmine has to say about it first."

"Mya? He's her husband, he has a right to know his wife is in danger."

"I know, but you forget how hot-tempered he can be. If I tell him he'll go looking for those men himself. This is a matter for the police to handle."

Mya and Gina return to the parlor. Jasmine's eyes remain fixed on the window.

"Are they gone?" Mya asks.

"Yeah, they're gone. They stood by the car talking for a moment. The short one made a phone call and then they left," Jasmine explains.

"Do you think they'll come back?"

"Hard to tell. Depends on how bad he wants those girls."

"Well, that's the thing, they're not here anymore. They went out the back door."

"Those poor girls, they're out there alone."

"What can the police do?"

"Not much really."

"They chased those girls in here. Can't you arrest them for that?"

"Did you hear them say they wanted to harm them?"

"You and I both know they did."

"It's not what you know but what you can prove."

"What about the guns they were carrying? The guns they pointed at us?"

"I think you should just drop it, Mya."

"What are you not telling me?"

"I recognized the short one. I think he's a Russian Mafia lieutenant. He's a dangerous man; very connected. The last police officer that arrested him wound up disappearing. So, I don't think you should try to press charges. I fear what might happen."

"I think it's a little too late to be cautious," Gina says.

"Not necessarily, this area is considered a safe zone. If the gangs honor the truce, maybe the Russian Mafia will too," Jasmine explains.

"What's gonna happen to those girls?" Mya asks.

"Attractive young ladies, they'll probably be sold as sex slaves," Jasmine says.

"Oh my God," Gina says.

"Jasmine, I hate to ask you this," Mya says.

"You don't have to; I'll go look for them. And if I find them, I'll take them to a safe place."

"Thank you, Jasmine. I'm gonna call Jed."

Chapter 14

Jedrek stops by the floral shop to pick up a fruit bouquet for Raisa. He remembers the first time he gave her one, and how excited she was to receive it. He knows his wife better than anyone, and he senses something is troubling her. Perhaps the sentiment will cheer her up.

"Hi, I'm Megan. How may I help you?" The florist asks.

"Hey Megan, I'd like to purchase a fruit bouquet, please.

"Any particular arrangement?"

Jedrek looks through the catalog on the counter.

"Last time I bought her the *'Fruit Festival'*. This time I think I'll go with the *'Doubly Delicious'*."

"Good choice. Will that be all for you today sir?"

"Yes, thank you."

"I've seen you before," she says preparing the bouquet.

"Probably, I've been here before."

"No, I don't think it was here. I just started working here a few weeks ago. It must have been somewhere else."

"Have you ever been to Mann's Auto Shop?"

"No."

"Well, you should go there and get your car serviced sometime."

"Are you a model?"

"No."

"Athlete?"

"No."

"Stripper?"

"Heck no."

Megan stares at Jedrek with dreamy eyes.

"Are you ok?" He asks.

"I'm sorry for staring. I'm just trying to figure out where I know you from. I could never forget a handsome face like yours."

"Thanks," he says awkwardly.

"So, is this bouquet for anyone special?"

"Yes, it's for my…"

"Because I would just love it if a man bought me a bouquet. Are you single?"

"I'm…"

"I'd like to get to know you."

"I'm…"

"I'll give you, my number. Maybe we could go out sometime."

"Miss, I'm married. The fruit bouquet is for my wife."

"Oh, you're married? Then why are you standing here flirting with me?"

Jedrek raises his hands out of confusion. Megan wraps the bouquet and places it on the counter.

"Here you go. Your total is $49.76, mister."

Jedrek reaches for his wallet.

"I'd love to meet your wife someday. To tell her you're going around flirting with other women."

Jedrek shakes his head and gives Megan a fifty-dollar bill.

"Keep the change, he says grabbing the bouquet."

"Thanks, cheapskate," she mutters.

Chapter 15

Raisa and Ashley exercise caution not to be seen. Raisa peeps around the corner of a building. The coast is clear; the pair make a break toward a side street. They duck behind a parked car when they hear an oncoming vehicle.

"It's a police car," Ashley says with delight.

Raisa tries to stop her from flagging the policeman down. The officer puts the car in park when he sees the girls.

"Is everything all right?" He asks stepping out of the car.

"Yes," Raisa says.

"No, we're being chased by some thugs," Ashley says.

"She's just joking," Raisa says.

"What are you doing?"

"We don't know if we can trust him," Raisa whispers.

"Hop in the car and I'll take you to the police station," the officer says.

"Shouldn't you radio for backup to help you catch those guys?" Ashley questions.

He smiles at them.

"He's already caught who he's looking for," Raisa says.

The man unholsters his sidearm.

"I insist you get in the car."

The ladies cooperate and get in the back seat.

"I'm sorry," Ashley says.

"I tried to warn you; they own the police."

"No one owns me. It's more of a partnership," the man explains.

He pulls out a cell phone and calls Laska.

"Hey, it's Arnold. I found what you were looking for. I'm behind the internet café. The one on Monroe…Sure thing."

He hangs up the phone.

"Daddy's on his way girls," he says with a chuckle.

"You're supposed to help people. Where is your honor?" Raisa asks.

"Honor? What would you know about honor? A woman that sells her body for money."

"We ran because we would not do such a thing. Those men tried to take us against our will," Raisa explains.

"You're here because you made the wrong choice somewhere down the line. Just like most women."

"Why do you wear that uniform, if you don't believe in justice?" Raisa asks.

"There was a time when I wanted to be a good cop. I tried to do everything by the book. I thought that making a difference was worth more than making a dollar. But one instance changed all that. In that same instance, I flushed my values down the drain...

"*My partner and I were called for a domestic disturbance. We'd been to that house before. Man gets drunk, acts disorderly, beats his wife, and scares the children. She never pressed charges. This time he took it too far. He had beaten her to a bloody pulp. We thought she'd had enough. We thought we finally had him. She wouldn't press charges; said it was her fault. We wanted to help her.*

"*So, my partner provoked him. He started insulting the man in front of his wife and kids. The man took the bait and punched my partner. We didn't need his wife to press charges. We had him for assaulting an officer. We roughed him up a little then cuffed him. His wife didn't like that. She told us to let him go, or she'd file a complaint against us. We refused to let him go. We told her it was for her protection.*

"*She picked up a hammer and attacked us. Before I could react, I was out cold. My partner wouldn't go down so easily, and he paid the price. He was so badly beaten he was hospitalized for weeks. All because we wanted to do the right thing and help someone who we thought was defenseless.*

"The woman stayed true to her word. She filed a complaint against our entire department. My partner and I were suspended while Internal Affairs investigated. The woman blamed us for the injuries she received from her husband. They said the woman acted in self-defense and no charges were filed. To avoid a lawsuit the department let us take the fall. Abuse of power, excessive force, and several other violations they stuck us with.

"We were left in the cold. No one would hire me. Which is how I ended up here in the mean streets of Tea Town. My partner sustained permanent brain damage. He'll never be able to work again.

"Sure, some people thought what we did was crooked. We knew that man was gonna kill that woman eventually. And we were right. A few months later he beat her to death in a drunken rage. So, where's the honor in that? You'll realize there is no justice in this world."

"You still have a chance to be a good cop; like you intended. Please let us go," Raisa pleads.

"Why would I wanna risk my neck protecting people too stupid to protect themselves? I figure you can let the streets run you, or you can run the streets."

"What if we were someone you cared about?" Raisa asks.

"Even if I had a conscience, I couldn't let you go. I'm in too deep. I stand to lose a lot if I help you. I'm sorry, I gotta look out for myself."

"I feel sorry for you."

"You feel sorry for me? You should feel sorry for yourself."

"May God have mercy on your soul."

"God? There is no God."

"Oh yes there is. Lest ye repent, ye shall also perish."

"Looks like you're gonna be the one on your knees begging. Here comes your master now."

Laska and Klavdii pull up behind the police car.

Chapter 16

"Gratitude Officer Arnold, for your efforts in capturing these two fugitives," Laska claps.

"Save your words and replace them with cash," Arnold says.

"What cash?"

"There should be a bounty for such a prize."

"You'll get your usual share."

"No, the price just went up. Turning a blind eye is one thing, but getting involved in the chase, getting my hands dirty. That's gonna cost you extra."

"Put it on my tab."

"Afraid not; that's cash on delivery comrade."

"How much?"

"Five grand."

"Done."

"Each."

"You're going to charge me a fee in exchange for my property?"

Klavdii racks the slide of his gun.

"Ten grand or you leave here empty-handed."

"Klavdii, give him the money."

Klavdii retrieves a leather satchel from the trunk of Laska's car. He pulls a stack of money from the bag and throws it at Arnold's feet.

"Here you are, your prime cuts of meat," Arnold says opening the car door.

"Get out!" Laska shouts at the timid ladies.

"A pleasure doing business with you," the officer says picking up the money.

"You have your 10 thousand. Now you must earn the money," Laska says.

"What are you talking about?" Arnold asks.

"There is a beauty shop about two blocks over. The women there need to be taught a lesson."

"What kind of lesson?"

"Torch it."

"No," Raisa says.

"I'm not doing that," Officer Arnold says.

Laska walks up to Arnold and holds a knife to his throat.

"You most certainly will, or I'll give you a happy face from ear to ear. Think about that the next time you try to muscle me for more money. Now get lost."

"Ok," Arnold says looking at Raisa, recalling her words.

"The officer gets in his car and drives away. Laska punches Raisa in the stomach. The blow knocks her to the ground.

"That's for costing me more money, you little whore."

Ashley cowers over Raisa.

"Help her up," Laska commands Ashley.

"Are you ok?" Ashley asks Raisa.

"I'll be fine," Raisa says.

"Get in the car," Laska orders.

Chapter 17

Raisa sits in the back seat wheezing and clenching her stomach.

"Quit your bellyaching, I didn't hit you that hard. You got off easy this time. I wouldn't want to bruise that pretty little face before the party," Laska says.

Ashley seated next to Raisa can no longer hold back her tears.

"Still yourself. Try not to let them see you crying. It only excites them even more," Raisa whispers.

"Where are they taking us?" Ashley asks wiping her eyes.

"You don't want to know."

"How can you be so calm at a time like this?"

"I have faith that God will see us through this."

"If God is gonna step in, what is He waiting for?"

"You have been presented with a choice. You can either give up or hold on to His unchanging hand."

"We'll never escape them, no matter how much we fight."

"All we can do is pray."

"Pray? What good is that?"

"Prayer can change anything; it can change everything. Never lose faith in Jesus."

"How has your faith helped you so far?"

"Just wait on Jesus. When the time comes, He will make a way."

"That's it? That's the only advice you have?"

"When we get there, tell them you're a virgin."

"But I'm not a virgin. What good would that do anyway?"

"Virgins are prized overall for their rarity. It will keep the men at bay for a while."

"What will happen to me if they find out I'm lying?"

"What are you whores whispering about? You're not plotting another escape are you, Raisa?" Laska asks.

"How did she escape the first time?" Klavdii asks.

"We were hosting a party for those cursed Black Gate Boys. There was an issue. One of those boys wasn't playing nice with one of our girls. I told Grigori to watch the girls while I went to see what the problem was. Galina was there with Grigori. She waited until I left the room. Then she hit Grigori with a vase, allowing Raisa to escape. By the time I was aware of what happened, Raisa managed to make it out of the hotel. I pursued her. She didn't get far, running around without shoes. She was trying to hide at a construction site when I cornered her. She picked up a brick and threw it."

"She threw a brick at you?" Klavdii laughs.

"No, she threw a brick at a passing car, shattering its windshield. The car turned out to be an unmarked police car."

"What are the odds?"

"I don't know, but the monkey arrested me."

"Why didn't you pay him off?"

"I tried, but he wasn't one of ours. He added bribery to my charges, along with public intoxication, destruction of property, and assault on an officer."

"You hit him?"

"Yes, he pissed me off."

"What did the cop say about Raisa?"

"He didn't see her. She ran after she threw the damn brick. I didn't even bother to mention her. It would've caused more trouble. He would've asked a lot of questions about her and the situation. It was bad enough having to straighten things out with Kazimir. I would not want to imagine if his operation had been compromised."

"Do you think she would have talked?"

"Yes, the whore's got balls, but she's not too big on brains. She didn't even bother to go into hiding. She made finding her too easy."

Laska turns to look at the frightened pair in the back seat.

"You're not the only one to make a bonehead mistake Raisa. Ashley here has daddy issues. She ran away from home because she couldn't deal with daddy's rules anymore. We found her hitchhiking on the side of the road. I bet you regret not accepting a ride from that old trucker. But don't worry, I'm your daddy now. Daddy's going to take good care of you."

"What will Kazimir think about all this?" Klavdii asks.

"What he doesn't know won't hurt him."

"Are you crazy? If we go against Kazimir we're dead."

Chapter 18

Jedrek tried to call Raisa upon leaving the floral shop. When she didn't answer, he assumed she was busy or taking a nap. He rushed home. He arrived to find the front door wide open.

"Raisa! I'm home baby. Where are you?"

He pauses at the sight of the broken vase shards scattered across the floor.

"What the…"

He sits the fruit bouquet on the console table.

"Raisa!"

He goes from room to room searching.

"Raisa! If this is a joke, please stop. It's not funny."

"Jed!" Mya exclaims entering the house.

"Mya! What are you doing here?"

"Jed, it's your wife. She's in trouble."

"What?"

"She came running into the salon earlier with another girl. They were being chased by two guys."

"Where's she now?"

"I don't know."

"What do you mean you don't know?"

"I hid them in the back room until the men left. When I went back to check on them, they were gone. They fled through the back door."

"Oh my God!"

Jedrek reaches for his phone. He tries to call Raisa again. He can hear her ringtone coming from the coffee table next to the couch. Shear panic grips his face when he glances at the phone.

"I gotta go find my wife. Tell me, Mya, what do these men look like?"

"I got my girl Jasmine out there looking for her. Just let the police handle it."

"Tell me!"

"One is of average height with blond hair. The other guy is taller with dark brown hair. From what Jasmine tells me they're Russian Mafiosos."

"Thank you."

"You know how dangerous it is to go after her."

"I don't care. If something's happened to her, I'm already dead," he says sprinting out the door.

"Jed be careful!"

Chapter 19

"Welcome to the Kremlin," Laska says.

They arrive at a hotel. The place is owned by the Russian Mafia boss. It's a business front for illegal gambling and prostitution. Laska points a gun at the ladies.

"No funny business or I guarantee you it will be the last mistake you make," he says.

He catches a glimpse of Raisa's hand.

"Who you were and what you were no longer holds meaning. The ring, give it to me," he commands.

"No," she says putting her hand behind her back.

"Give me the ring or we will take the whole finger."

Klavdii presents his bowie knife. Raisa takes off the ring and hands it to Laska.

"Good girl," he says putting the ring in his inner coat pocket.

Laska gets out first. He grabs the rear passenger door handle on Ashley's side. Ashley buries her head in Raisa's chest and holds on to her tight.

"No! No!" Ashley shouts.

Laska grabs her by the hair.

"Don't hurt her," Raisa pleads.

Laska unhands her. He points the gun at Raisa.

"Get out of the car now, or I will show no mercy."

Raisa gently rubs Ashley's hair.

"It will be ok. I won't let anything happen to you."

"You promise?" Ashley asks with teary eyes.

"I promise."

"Aww! Isn't that sweet? The little whore has a guardian angel," Klavdii says.

"A miracle on dirty whore street," Laska smirks.

Ashley steps out of the car with Raisa close to her heels. Laska grabs Ashley and puts his arm around her neck.

"Raisa promises to keep you safe. She has no control over what happens to you, I do…Come, let's go meet our guest."

Laska walks with his arm around Ashley and Klavdii with a tight grip around Raisa's arm.

"This must be like déjà vu for you Raisa. Considering tonight's guests are the Black Gate Boys. You see Ashley there is a truce between the gangs in Tea Town. If one wishes to move product through a gang's turf, he must pay for the privilege. The gang gets a nice percentage from the product distribution. Everyone wins.

"We throw them a party to cement the deal. The cost of the party is subtracted from the percentage they receive. Our boss is old and set in his ways. If it were up to me, I'd take the territories by force. Then I'd tax the gangs and kill anyone that stood in my way."

Laska opens the door, and they enter the main lobby. They walk by the front desk. A short man wearing bifocals with a terrible comb-over nods at Laska. A nod to inform him that everything is going well. Laska nods in response. The man stares at Raisa and in a sickening display, he licks his lips at her. Raisa looks away. The elevator doors open, and they get in.

"Press the button for the sixth floor," Laska instructs Ashley.

Ashley presses the button with a trembling finger. Raisa now thinks about Jedrek. She wonders if she'll ever see her love again. She also worries about the fate that awaits her on the sixth floor. As the elevator climbs to the sixth floor, the sound of loud rap music can be heard in the distance.

The elevator dings to announce they've reached their destination. The doors open to booming bass and a cloud of marijuana smoke. The clamoring of men in the near distance is overshadowed by the cries of women screaming. The commotion only fuels the preexisting anxiety Raisa and Ashley share. Laska proceeds to take Ashley down the hall with Klavdii and Raisa following closely. They draw near two men talking outside room 6C.

"What do we have here?" A man with a black baseball cap asks before puffing a blunt.

Another guy sitting in a gray foldable chair reaches for the blunt. The man in the black hat boldly gropes Ashley's breast. The unwanted touch startles her.

"Not this one, she's just here to watch," Laska says.

"Oh, my bad," the man says moving his hand.

"This one is ready to play," Laska motions his head to Raisa.

"Is that right? Come here girl," the man in the foldable chair says grabbing Raisa and pulling her closer.

Ashley watches in horror as the man forces Raisa onto his lap. Raisa closes her eyes. The man holds her tight with both hands. He blows smoke in her face.

"Gimme the blunt Rell," the guy in the fitted hat says snatching the blunt from his mouth.

"You smell good baby," Rell tries to suck on Raisa's neck. She jerks her head forward.

"Where'd you get this one from?" She too fine to be a hoe, Rell says."

The man in the black hat notices Raisa is frowning with her eyes closed.

"You don't like him, baby? Is that it? You want Hype to go first, don't you?" He asks rubbing her face.

"I'm going first," Rell says pulling Raisa closer.

The door to 6D opens and Rafiq emerges.

"Ra! I didn't know you were going to be here," Laska says.

Rafiq looks at Ashley.

"Your recruiting is getting sloppy. This one looks like a kid."

"Hey, I don't tell you how to run your business do I? I thought you hated these parties anyway?"

"I do. I'm just stopping through to make sure everything is all good. I was just on my way out."

"What were you doing in that room? Were you enjoying the festivities?"

"Hell no! I had to holla at Burn about something. He'll be in charge in my absence."

Laska glances over at Burn, standing in the doorway of 6D with a gun in his hand. Laska smirks.

"Take your shirt off hoe!" Rell exclaims tugging at Raisa's shirttail.

Rafiq sees Raisa and recognizes her instantly. Rafiq looks at Laska who's focused his attention back on Rell.

"She likes it rough," Laska tells him.

"Oh really," Rell replies.

Rafiq reaches around Laska and grabs Raisa's hand.

"I'm going first," he says yanking Raisa from Rell's lap.

"Raisa opens her eyes and looks at the floor.

"I thought you weren't in a partying mood Ra," Laska prods.

"This one looks too good to pass up," Rafiq explains.

"That's messed up Ra," Rell stands in anger.

"Excuse me, what did you say?" Rafiq asks.

"Nothing Ra," Rell raises his hands in surrender.

"That's what I thought."

Hype laughs at Rell.

"Shut the hell up," Rell says to Hype.

"Why didn't you say that to Ra?" Hype asks.

"I don't care. I'ma go in Tech room and snatch that little blonde from him."

Rell and Hype go into room 6B. Rafiq leads Raisa to 6D.

"You don't want to miss this," Laska says to Ashley.

Rafiq looks at Burn standing in the doorway.

"Anyone tries to open this door, shoot them," he tells Burn.

Rafiq closes the door behind him. Burn stands in front of the door and cocks the hammer of his gun while facing Laska.

"Private party," Burn says.

"Man wants his privacy. I can respect that."

Laska forces Ashley into 6B.

Chapter 20

Jedrek parks his car in front of the salon. He races around to the alleyway. He looks around but he can't find a clue as to which direction Raisa may have gone. Just when all hope seems lost. Jedrek almost steps on a rotten banana. A shoe imprint is embedded in the smushed banana.

It could be Raisa's footprint. It reminds him of the pair of UGG slippers he gave her. He recalls the time he bought them. How Raisa's reaction was anticlimactic. She said she would never spend that much money on a pair of slippers. He looks around and notices scattered fragments of the banana.

Perhaps they're traces Raisa left behind. It's a long shot but it's all he has to go on. The tracks lead in the opposite direction from which he came. The trail goes cold as he makes it out of the alley and into the street.

"They stop here. What does that mean? C'mon Lord, please show me a sign. Don't let it end like this," he says looking up.

A car pulls up. Jedrek is blinded by the high beams. He uses his hand to shelter his eyes from the light. The driver stops the car and dims the lights. Officer Arnold steps out of the car.

"What are you doing back here buddy?" Arnold asks.

"Officer I'm looking for my wife."

"You expect me to believe that?"

"It's the truth."

"Is that your car in front of the store with the engine running?"

"I was in such a hurry I guess I forgot."

"Yeah, right pal. Why don't you show me some I.D.?"

"I don't have time for this," Jedrek says turning around.

"Don't you walk away from me!"

"Am I under arrest? Because I didn't do anything."

"What I have is probable cause. Your vehicle left idling in front of the store and you, snooping around the back. Seems suspicious to me; probably trying to find a way to break in."

"And do what? Steal haircare products? It's a salon, not a bank. Look, if you don't have a real reason to arrest me. I'ma go now."

"Damn right you're going. You're going with me downtown."

"Man, I'm just trying to find my wife!"

"And if that's true you don't have anything to worry about. Unless you want me to charge you with conspiracy to commit theft."

"This is bull crap, and you know it."

"Turn around."

Arnold handcuffs Jedrek.

"Is this necessary? I'm not resisting."

"Shut up, or anything you say can and will be used against you in a court of law."

"Just listen to me, officer. Do you normally patrol this area?"

"No, but today it's been really popular."

"Did you see a woman around here earlier?"

"No, I haven't seen them."

"Wait, I never said she was with anyone."

Officer Arnold hits Jedrek in the back of the head. Jedrek falls to his knees and then onto his left side.

"You couldn't leave well enough alone, could you? Laska told me to come back and torch this place down to the ground. Send those little black tramps a message; that this is what happens when you don't mind your own business. Then you show up, perfect timing.

"I'll burn this place down and say you did it. I'll tell everyone you went for my gun when I caught you. I had no choice but to shoot you. I'll be a hero and you'll be the idiot that fell in love with a whore."

Jedrek rolls over to see Arnold pointing a gun at him.

"Any last words before you die?"

"Go to hell."

"After I shoot you, I'm gonna go bone your wife."

Jedrek kicks Arnold's left kneecap causing it to bend in the opposite direction. He falls but manages to squeeze off a shot, narrowly missing Jedrek's head. The gun slips from Arnold's grasp, but Jedrek's hands are cuffed behind his back. He can't grab the gun, nor can he get up fast enough to run. Arnold crawls toward the gun. Without hesitation Jedrek kicks Arnold in the face, knocking him out cold. He kicks him again for good measure.

"That's for my wife."

Another car pulls up beside Arnold's squad car. Jedrek believes it's another police car.

"Oh crap, now how am I gonna get outta this?"

"Jed," a woman says.

"Jasmine is that you?"

"Yeah, it's me, Jed."

"Oh, thank God. Can you get me outta these cuffs?"

"I see you met public enemy number one," she says looking at Arnold.

She helps Jedrek to his feet and takes the handcuffs off him.

"Thank you, he was gonna kill me. I think he knows where my wife is."

"He'll die before you get him to talk."

"How did you know I was here?"

"Mya called me. She's really worried about you and for good reason. These people that are after your wife; you don't wanna mess with them."

"They don't wanna mess with me."

"I know I can't stop you from searching for your wife but try to be careful. I have a few of my buddies keeping an eye out for her too."

"Are you sure you can trust them? I mean, look at this guy." Jedrek says pointing at Arnold.

"Don't worry about him. I got something for him. If I hear anything about your wife, I'll let you know."

"Thanks."

Jedrek runs back to his car and drives off. Jasmine looks down at Arnold.

"Piece of trash," she says while ripping the badge off his uniform.

Chapter 21

"You can open your eyes now," Rafiq tells Raisa.

"I don't want to look at you."

Raisa sits at the foot of the bed as Rafiq stands over her.

"It's all right; just open your eyes."

"No."

"Have it your way."

Rafiq jumps on the bed.

"Can you pass me the remote?"

Raisa turns to see Rafiq fully clothed laying on the bed.

"What?"

"The remote, can you pass it to me? I wanna see if the game is on."

Raisa gets up and grabs the TV remote from the countertop and hands it to Rafiq.

"Thank you. You can relax I'm not gonna hurt you."

"Why should I believe you?"

"You're right, you don't have a reason to trust me. It's no secret you don't wanna be here. I know all you girls are here against your will. I know you're married."

"How did you know that?"

Rafiq points at Raisa's ring finger.

"I see the spot where your wedding band was. Your husband must be worried sick about you."

Raisa displays a worried look at the thought of Jedrek being in pain.

"Do you love him?"

"With all my heart."

"Then I'll do my damnedest to reunite you with him," Rafiq smiles.

"How will you do that?"

"Don't worry, I have a plan. In the meantime, we'll sit here and pretend like we're doing it."

Two doors down the Black Gate Boys take advantage of a helpless young lady. The woman stares blankly into space; completely zoned out. While the three gang members roughly handle her. The woman barely moves or makes a sound. She's at the mercy of the disgusting trio and whatever drug she's been given.

"That could be you. Would you like to trade places with her?" Laska whispers to Ashley.

"No, I'm a virgin," Ashley replies.

"You lie."

"I am, I swear."

Laska ogles her hips.

"You're mighty healthy for one who has never been touched."

"I'm Hispanic, most of us have curves."

"You know if you're lying to me, you'll be punished."

Laska places his hand on Ashley's waist and unbuttons her pants.

"Ok, I'm not a virgin but don't punish me. I only lied because I'm afraid. I'll do whatever you say."

"I'm sure you will."

Laska grabs Ashley by the throat.

"If you lie to me again…"

"I won't, I swear."

He relents

"Let's go, I have big plans for you."

He puts his arm around her shoulders and motions her toward the door. Ashley looks back at the tortured woman. She notices a single tear rolling down the side of her face. Laska turns Ashley around and sweeps her out of the room.

Chapter 22

"What's this plan of yours?" Raisa asks Rafiq.

"In a few minutes, I'm gonna open that door and tell Laska I'm keeping you for the night."

"Do you believe that will work?"

"He'll agree to it. I can be very persuasive."

"And then?"

"After he leaves, I'll take you back to your husband."

"Why are you helping me? What do you get out of it?"

"You might find this hard to believe but I'm really a nice guy."

Raisa gives Rafiq a look of doubt.

"If you want to prove you're a nice guy. You should help the other women escape too."

"And how would I do that?"

"Your people outnumber Laska's. You could take the girls by force if you wanted to."

"You're not thinking this through. Suppose he won't let the girls go without a fight. Sure, my people would win today but not without consequence. Suppose you or one of those other girls got caught in a crossfire. That wouldn't be good for anyone.

"Then there's the threat of retaliation. It would start a gang war. One, my people can't win. Believe me, I've thought about it several times. I know you don't trust me, but you have to. My plan might be the only shot we have; without getting anyone killed."

"Ok, we will go with your plan. But what happens after you take me back to my husband?"

"I'll tell Laska you escaped. Then you and your husband have to get outta town."

"And go where?"

"As far as possible and never come back."

Rafiq looks at Raisa sympathetically.

"It's the only way y'all will be safe."

Raisa nods her head. Rafiq stands up and extends his hand to Raisa.

"It's showtime."

Raisa takes his hand and stands up.

"Now you're gonna have to be convincing when we go out there. I need you to look as sad as you did when you came in here."

"I don't think I can. I'm too nervous. He will see right through me."

Rafiq puts his hands on Raisa's shoulders.

"Think about never seeing your husband again, because that's exactly what's gonna happen if we don't get this right."

Raisa's eyes begin to tear up.

"That's the look I'm going for."

Rafiq grabs Raisa by the hand and walks to the door.

"Look down at the floor, like you're ashamed."

He opens the door. Burn looks at Rafiq.

"All good Ra?"

"Yeah man, it's all good."

Laska and Ashley are waiting in the hallway.

"Well, it's about time. I thought you were trying to go for a marathon," Laska complains.

"I couldn't help myself. She was so good," Rafiq boasts.

"Yeah, she's high-class stuff."

"I was hoping you would let me hold on to her for the night."

"I don't think that would be such a good idea; maybe some other time."

"I don't think it's too much to ask for an all-nighter with one of your best. Kazimir owes me anyway."

"How do you figure?"

"Do you think I'm stupid? I know Kazimir cheats us outta money by throwing these parties. The only reason I go along with it is that my boys get a kick out of it."

"Kazimir is not here right now. Therefore, you deal with me directly."

"No, he isn't here but he knows if I'm unsatisfied about anything; the deal is off. Do you wanna be the one to tell him that I'm unsatisfied?"

"Fine, keep the slut for one night. Ashley and I have plans."

Laska leans over and kisses Ashley on the cheek. Raisa looks up at Ashley and sees the fear in her eyes. The whole time Raisa's been preoccupied with the thought of going home. She forgot about the promise she made to poor little Ashley.

"Let's go, Ashley," Laska says.

"Wait, don't leave me here," Raisa appeals to Laska."

"You're staying with me baby," Rafiq says.

"Please take me with you," Raisa's eyes stay fixed on Ashley.

Rafiq looks at Ashley and then Raisa. Laska smiles.

"Come to me Raisa," Laska says with an inviting hand gesture.

Burn moves out the way to let Raisa pass. Rafiq grabs Raisa's hand. She looks at him and mouths the word no. Rafiq gives her a puzzled look. Laska looks at Rafiq.

"She doesn't want to stay with you Ra. Are you going to make her stay against her will?"

"No," Rafiq says letting go of her hand.

Raisa embraces Ashley.

"I guess she's had enough black meat for one day. Now she will have a real man," Laska says.

"You're not a real man; you're a pervert," Rafiq responds.

"Who are you calling pervert?" Klavdii asks.

"Give me a reason," Burn says holding his gun.

"We may have a truce but let me remind you. Your little gang is not prepared to go to war with us," Laska jeers.

"You hide behind Kazimir," Rafiq says.

"One day Kazimir will have no more use for you. When that day comes, I hope I'm the one to put a bullet in your head."

"Just say the word Ra," Burn says pointing his gun.

"Stand down Burn," Rafiq says lowering Burn's gun.

"Are we done Ra?" Laska asks.

"Yeah, we're done, but this ain't over."

"Oh, but it is. It was over for you the moment you insulted me. Be sure to watch your back."

"You do what you gotta do to mend your wounded pride. But you know as well as I do; you can't make a move against me without Kazimir's consent. So, go on with your veil threats."

"I grow tired of this exchange. Let's go," Laska tugs Ashley away from Raisa."

They walk back to the elevator; Laska with Ashley and Klavdii with Raisa, just as they entered.

"Klavdii, I want you to remain here with Bruno. To make sure there are no more issues with these Black Gate Boys," Laska instructs.

"Sure thing, I'll meet you at the spot later."

Laska boards the elevator with his two captives.

Klavdii and Bruno stand at the end of the hall. Raisa looks at Rafiq as the elevator doors close. He lifts his hands in confusion.

"I hope you know what you're doing," Rafiq whispers.

Inside the elevator, Laska stares at Raisa with malicious intent.

"Do you think I'll go easy on you because you begged to come with me? What, are you trying to gain my favor? Or do you still believe you're going to protect Ashley from me? Either way, the fact remains you undermined my authority, by disobeying a direct order. You made me look bad in front of those monkeys. Like I don't have my house in order. You will follow my commands. Do you understand?"

"Yes," Raisa answers.

"Yes, what?"

"Yes…master."

"That's better."

Chapter 23

"You should've let me blast that fool," Burn says tucking his gun in the back of his pants.

"She may have gotten killed in the crossfire," Rafiq explains.

"Who are you talking about; that girl you were with? Yeah, she was fly. I wouldn't wanna see anything happen to such a beauty. What's on your mind bro? You, planning something?"

"I'm still thinking about how to approach this. In the meantime, you round up the boys and meet me downstairs. This party is over."

"Done," Burn says with a grin.

"I gotta go help my brother."

Rafiq proceeds to walk down the hall.

"Party's over!" Burn shouts and pounds on the doors.

"One of these days someone is gonna burn this place down to the ground. And I hope like hell Laska is in here when that happens," Rafiq says walking by Klavdii.

Klavdii ignores Rafiq and directs his attention to the half-naked women exiting the rooms. The women line up outside the rooms; awaiting Bruno to put their shackles on. Klavdii notices he's a woman short. The Black Gate boys begin to leave the hotel. Burn along with a few; take the elevator. While the majority take the stairs. Klavdii walks into 6B and sees the short blonde woman on the bed.

"Get up," he demands.

The woman does not move a muscle. She stares mindlessly at the ceiling.

"I said get up!" He smacks the right side of her face.

A needle falls on the floor. Klavdii looks at the needle. Then he checks the woman's pulse.

"Great, this is just what I need."

Klavdii walks out of the room and sees Bruno shackling the girls to prepare them for transport.

"What is it?" Bruno looks up.

"That slut OD'd."

"She's free now; good for her," a woman with dark hair says.

"Do you think this is funny?" Klavdii steps forward.

"Yeah, let's see you try to have sex with her now," the woman laughs.

"Klavdii punches the woman bloodying her nose. The woman falls to the floor along with the girl she's shackled to.

"We should call Laska," Bruno suggests.

"We can handle this ourselves. Let's get them to the house. Then we'll come back for the other girl. In the meantime, tell that idiot at the front desk not to let anyone on this floor."

Klavdii closes the door to 6B.

Chapter 24

"Stop swerving you dumb slag!" Laska yells at Raisa from the back seat.

"I don't know how to drive," she says trembling.

"You better not wreck my car, or sweet cheeks here might catch a bullet in the head," Laska points the gun at Ashley's temple.

"I'll drive carefully, please take the gun away from her head."

"You have feelings for this girl. I think I'll leave the gun where it is for now. Whatever you're planning, rethink it. If you dare defy me, I'll take it out on her. So, don't mess up; for Ashley's sake."

Raisa manages to concentrate on the road and steadies the car.

"Turn left at the next stoplight," Laska instructs.

Raisa contemplates how to help Ashley escape. She does not want the girl to go through what she went through. Those are memories that will haunt her for perhaps a lifetime.

"I said turn left stupid!" Laska hits the back of Raisa's headrest with the butt of the gun.

"I'm sorry," Raisa says slowing down.

"Leave her alone, she's trying," Ashley chimes in.

Laska backhands Ashley in the mouth.

"Did I tell you to speak?"

"Hang on Ashley. I won't let him hurt you anymore," Raisa thinks to herself, looking at Ashley in the rearview mirror.

"Pay attention, Raisa. I'm only going to tell you once. You missed the last turn. You will have to make a right turn here, then go back around."

Raisa does as she is told.

"Good, now follow this street to the very end."

Raisa remembers visiting the upscale neighborhood. Jedrek showed her houses there and talked about buying one someday and having children. Jedrek her man, how she longs to be reunited with him. But she made a sacrifice for Ashley. Something she feels Jedrek would've done. At the end of the road is a "dead end" sign. Raisa stops the car and waits for further instructions.

"Keep going," he says.

The street curves around a small patch of trees. The pavement ends as Raisa turns into the curve onto a rock path. There at the very end of the road sits an awesome duplex.

"Pull up to the front door," Laska commands.

Raisa knows it's now or never. She parks the car and turns the engine off.

"Raisa, I want you to get out first and open my door. No heroics or Ashley is a goner."

Raisa gets out of the car slowly; not to excite Laska. She gently opens Laska's door. He grabs the top of the car door with his left hand and pulls himself up, planting his left foot on the ground first. Raisa watches his movements closely. The moment he plants his right foot on the ground. She notices the gun is no longer pointed at Ashley. Without a second thought, she grabs Laska and puts him in a chokehold; forcing him to drop the gun.

"Run Ashley!" Raisa screams.

Ashley hurriedly climbs out of the back seat and runs around the car. She stops and glances over at Raisa.

"Go!" Raisa hollers.

Laska spins around and bumps Raisa into the open car door, knocking her to the ground. He picks up the gun and points it at Ashley, who's running toward the backyard. He looks down at Raisa.

"She won't get far. Get up."

"Or what, you will punish me?"

"No, get up or I'll send someone to kill your husband. And you know I will do it. Now get your ass up," he grabs her by the hair and forces her onto her feet. He pulls her inside the house and takes her to a room. Then he pushes her inside a large animal cage and slams the door shut.

"Don't you lay a hand on that girl, you sick twisted freak," Raisa says.

"What did you call me?"

"You heard me."

"You're trying to provoke me; to distract me from pursuing Ashley. Like I told you before, you disobey me and I'll take it out on her…Oh, and to show you how sick and twisted I am. When I get back, you and I are going to make a video. Then I'm going to send a copy to your husband."

"You bastard!" She spits in his face.

He wipes the spit from his face and licks his fingers.

"I'm going to enjoy ripping you to pieces. But for now, I must go find Ashley. Wish me luck.

Raisa looks away.

"When I return, lights camera action. I hope you like whips and chains. We will see if you can still hit those high notes like you used to."

Laska leaves the house. Raisa hears the front door slam close. She looks around the cage for a weak spot, a way out. She rattles the cage a little and the door pops open.

"He left in such a hurry. He forgot to lock it."

Her first thought is to search for a phone but no luck. She flees the house but stops to think. Knowing Laska is hunting Ashley. Knowing he might catch her. Knowing Laska won't stop coming after her.

Knowing he's willing to hurt Jedrek to keep her in line. Raisa decides to stay and fight. She goes back into the house to find something she can use as a weapon. She goes to the kitchen and grabs a knife.

"Too short."

She would have to get close enough to use a knife. Laska was smart enough not to leave any guns lying in the open.

"There has to be something better than this knife."

She recalls seeing a fireplace in the family room. She goes back to the room and grabs a fire poker.

"This time I will be waiting for you, you creep," she taps her left palm with the fire poker.

Chapter 25

"This is Jedrek; leave your name, number, and a brief message and I'll get back to you as soon as possible."

Rafiq listens to Jedrek's personalized greeting for the third time.

"C'mon Jed, pick up the phone," Rafiq says in frustration.

He dials again.

"Hello?" Jedrek answers.

"It's about time you answered."

"Ra? I don't know who gave you, my number. But I'm not in the mood nor do I have time to talk to you."

"Jed it's about your wife."

"Do you know where she is?"

"Yeah, I do."

"Where is she?!"

"The Russians have her."

"You've seen her?"

"Yes."

"And you didn't try to help her?"

"I did! I talked to her. I told her I'd help her. I had a plan and everything. She was down for it, but at the last minute, she decided to go back with them. I think it had something to do with the other girl that was with them."

"What girl?"

"Some Mexican looking girl, probably underage."

"Must've been the girl Mya saw her with earlier. Do you know where they are now?"

"I have an idea. It's one or two places he could've taken her."

"Where are they?"

"One is on Hoover. It's a basement flat next to a recording studio."

"And the other one?"

"A duplex in an upscale part of town, Cherry Heights I think."

"Do you have an address for it?"

"I hear it's the last house on the road, can't miss it."

"Thanks."

"Jed, there's no way you can be in two places at once. Burn and I will go to the flat, and I'll send my boys to meet you at Cherry Heights."

"No thanks. I plan on handling this myself."

"By yourself? I know you're angry right now but you're not thinking clearly. It's suicide to go alone. You're my brother and I don't wanna see anything happen to you. Please let us help you."

"Thanks for the info, bro," Jedrek ends the call.

"Jed?! Jed?! That fool's gonna get himself killed."

"He made his choice. What can you do? You gotta give him props for wanting to put in his own work though," Burn says.

"Jed's grandmother took me in when I was an orphan, and they treated me like family. He went to jail because he wouldn't snitch on me. He's one of the best people I know. He doesn't deserve any of this. I'll be damned if I let him die."

"You're willing to go against the Russians to help him?"

"I'll die protecting him. Are you with me?"

"Brother, you already know. I'll go through the fire with you."

"Good, 'cause if we die tonight; we're going straight to hell."

"Where to?"

"To Hoover and gun it. We need to get there before Jed."

Chapter 26

Ashley ran and hid in the shrubbery behind the house. She waited and listened for a shot, but it never came. Instead, she heard the commotion Laska made dragging Raisa into the house.

"I can't just leave her. She risked her life to save me," Ashley says.

Ashley runs into the wooded area behind the house. She circles around through the trees; back to the houses, they passed on the way in. She comes to the back of a house with a huge pit bull. The dog growls at Ashley.

"Nice doggo, please don't hurt me. I'm just passing through."

The dog charges at her.

"Oh, fudge!" She yells.

Ashley is paralyzed with fear. She closes her eyes. The dog stops two feet away from her legs; barking uncontrollably. Ashley opens her eyes and sees the dog is hindered by a chain. She breathes a sigh of relief and laughs.

"Screw you, pooch."

She heads for the front of the house. She steps with caution, making sure to avoid the dog. She rings the doorbell and waits for someone to answer. A minute goes by, and she rings the doorbell again. Anxious and frustrated, Ashley kicks the door.

"Open the damn door! I need help! I know someone's home I can see the light on."

Ashley watches as the light goes out.

"What the hell?! Look if you're not gonna open the door, at least call the police. Or better yet call the FBI, because the police around here suck."

She kicks the door again.

"Screw you then!"

She leaves the house. She looks at the big house to her left and notices the lights are off.

"I could've sworn those lights were on a second ago."

Ashley looks at the houses farther down the road and sees there are no lights on.

"What the hell? There's something odd about this neighborhood."

The place is suspiciously quiet, aside from the dog she encountered. She didn't hear any other animals or insects for that matter. Although Ashley is terrified of bugs, she wondered what place on earth doesn't have mosquitoes? Ashley sees a shadow behind a curtain in the house across the street. She dashes to the house and rings the doorbell.

"Please help me! I know someone is in there. I saw you watching me from the window."

"There you are Ashley," Laska approaches.

Ashley turns around to see Laska pointing a gun at her from a short distance. She panics and bangs on the door.

"Please help me!"

"Shh!" Laska utters with his index finger pressed to his lips.

The door opens.

"What is the meaning of this?" Asks an older man with a white woolly beard.

"Help, he's gonna kill me!" Ashley responds.

"Everything's under control Mr. Corwin," Laska says inching closer.

"I beg to differ, Laska. This girl is likely to wake the dead."

The man grabs Ashley by the arm and shoves her into Laska.

"Shut her up immediately."

"Please don't let him take me," Ashley pleads.

"Thank you, Mr. Corwin. I'm sorry for the inconvenience," Laska says.

"You need to learn to control your pets, Laska."

"You old douchebag," Ashley says.

"You're lucky you're not my type, or you'd pay for that remark," Corwin says.

"I'll just take my slave and go now," Laska puts the gun to Ashley's hip.

"As President of the Homeowner's Association, the people of Cherry Heights rely on me to be their voice. I think I speak for everyone by saying, get your stuff together Laska or you're out of here. You of all people should appreciate the lengths we go to preserve our anonymity, Goodnight."

"Goodnight Mr. Corwin."

Corwin goes back into the house and closes the door. Laska forcefully removes Ashley from Corwin's doorstep.

"You said you would do whatever I say. You lied to me, Ashley."

"I'm sorry, it won't happen again," she says trembling.

"I don't believe you."

He stops in the middle of the road.

"On your knees."

"What?"

"Get on your knees."

Ashley kneels in front of Laska.

"Beg for your life, little flower."

"Please don't kill me."

"Is that the best you can do? I don't think you understand the seriousness of this. Your life is at stake."

"I beg you please spare my life. I'll do whatever you say, I promise."

"I'm not convinced, open your mouth."

Ashley opens her mouth wide. Laska puts the gun in her mouth.

"Now, I want to hear you beg for your life."

The door to a large brick house with burgundy shutters opens. A short middle-aged woman steps out.

"I wanna watch you kill her. Kill the filthy harlot."

Ashley looks over at the woman and sees her smiling.

Ashley begins to sob profusely. She starts choking; trying to get her words out with the barrel resting on her tongue. Laska laughs at the spectacle.

"I'm sorry to disappoint you, Mrs. Dawson. There will be no execution tonight. Ashley has learned her lesson."

"You got me all excited for nothing," the woman says going back into her home.

Laska pulls Ashley to her feet.

"No one cares about you Ashley. You'll realize there are worse things in this world than me. Everyone here in Cherry Heights has a vice; for Corwin, it's little boys. Mrs. Dawson and her husband like to make snuff films.

"If you or Raisa resist me again, I'll gladly hand you over to one of my neighbors. I guarantee you they're not as nice as I am. You caused a scene tonight, but it was Raisa that created a diversion. I promise I won't be gentle with her; not like before. You get to watch and clean up after I'm done."

Chapter 27

"I will strike him in the head the moment he walks through the door," Raisa murmurs to herself.

She struggles to control her breathing as anxiety sets in.

"Get it together girl; don't want to be too anxious. You only have one shot at this," she exhales."

She knows any misstep could ruin the whole plan. Someone approaches; this is it. The moment she's been waiting for. It's all or nothing. The doorknob slowly turns, and the door slowly creaks open.

Raisa readily waits behind the door; fire poker clutched tight in hand. There's no turning back now. The door completely opens. Raisa quietly steps back to avoid being hit by the door.

Laska comes in humming. He clasps the door's edge and pushes to close it. With a loud shriek, Raisa lunges from behind the door; fire poker in mid-swing. She pauses at the sight of Ashely, narrowly missing her with the fire poker.

"Oh gosh!" She says.

Laska pushes Ashely into Raisa causing them both to topple over. Raisa loses her grip on the fire poker. Laska kicks it away before Raisa can reach for it. Ashley trips Laska making him drop his gun. The gun slides across the floor. Laska sees Raisa going after the fire poker. He grabs her by the hair.

"Get up," he commands.

Ashley grabs the gun and points it at Laska. He takes out a knife and holds it to Raisa's throat.

"Go ahead shoot and send us both to hell. You don't have the heart girl, do you?"

"But I do," Jedrek says standing in the doorway.

"Jeed!" Raisa excites.

"Let my wife go."

"The husband, you've got balls coming here. A waste of time coming here to save a whore."

"Watch your mouth," Jedrek warns.

"Or you'll do what? You're no bad man. I can see it in your eyes. A lowly mechanic, a servant of the people. Me, I'm a king. The people serve me. Your wife serves me. You should know your darling wife has sex with other men for money.

"She had fun with another man tonight. She pleased him so well that he begged me to keep her. Now you come in here waving a gun like you're tough. If you were a real man, we wouldn't be talking. You're a sissy and I'll prove it."

Laska applies pressure to the knife against Raisa's throat. Jedrek grits his teeth and the gun judders in his hand.

"Jeed, don't do it," Raisa cries.

"Stop him!" Ashely screams.

"How much?" Jedrek asks.

"How much what?" Laska asks.

"How much money to make you go away?"

"How much do you have?"

"What are you doing?" Ashley asks Jedrek.

"I'm doing what I have to. Fifty thousand dollars. It's all yours if you let my wife go and never bother her again."

"Fifty thousand dollars, for this whore?"

"Do we have a deal?" Jedrek asks with an angry tone.

"We have a deal."

Laska releases Raisa. She runs to Jedrek and hugs him tight.

"Jeed!"

Ashley keeps the gun on Laska.

"Don't, it'll haunt you if you pull that trigger," Jedrek says to Ashley.

Ashley lowers the gun. Laska snickers.

"I love this country. I kidnap your wife and put her to work, then you pay me for my trouble. This is your knight and shining armor Raisa? The one you were afraid for? He is not worthy of respect; he is no man."

"Go and wait for me in the car. There's one more thing I must do," Jedrek says to Raisa.

"Jeed let's just go," she grabs his arm.

"I promise I'll be right there."

"Come on," Ashley grabs Raisa's hand and guides her to the door.

Raisa stops to look back at Jedrek.

"It's ok, I just wanna iron out the details," he says to her.

"I'll see you around Raisa," Laska taunts.

Raisa gives Laska a death stare as she walks out.

"She is a pistol that one, but of course, you know that," Laska says.

Jedrek stares Laska down.

"Is there something else you wish to say to me? If not, you are free to leave my house to go get my money. I'll contact you tomorrow and tell you where to drop it off. Remember Mr. Mechanic I don't play. Tomorrow I'll be there to collect; the money or the girl."

"Yeah, I see how it is."

"You're pretty smart for a monkey."

"It's an American custom that we shake hands when we make a deal."

Jedrek puts the gun away and steps forward. Laska smiles and steps forward.

"It is a Russian custom as well."

They shake hands. Jedrek squeezes Laska's hand so hard it pops. Jedrek pulls Laska in close and headbutts him. Laska is stunned. Jedrek headbutts him again, knocking him to the floor.

"Did you really think I was gonna let you get away with that? Fool, I was never gonna make a deal with you. I just said all that crap to get my wife outta here safe. Plus, I don't want her to see what happens next."

Jedrek kicks him in the face.

"She's not a violent person. She made me promise I'd stay outta trouble. It hurts to break that promise."

Laska tries to crawl away.

"Where do you think you're going?"

Jedrek stomps his back. Laska grunts in agony.

"Don't leave before you receive your payback."

Jedrek stomps him again.

"If you stop now, I promise I'll make your death quick," Laska coughs up blood.

"That can't be good. You might have some internal bleeding. You should see a doctor."

Jedrek stomps his back again.

"A real man doesn't terrorize women. A real man protects them."

"You're weak."

"Yeah, I am because I let someone like you drag me to this point."

Jedrek stomps his right arm shattering several bones. Laska groans.

"Do you think this will make a difference? Your wife is still a whore no matter how badly you beat me."

"My wife is a queen."

Jedrek kicks Laska in the ribs. Laska lets out a loud gasp for air.

"That had to hurt. I heard them crack," Jedrek laughs.

"You're a dead man; you and your entire family. I guarantee it."

"Your threats won't work on me. You and your friends like to hurt women. I wanna hear you beg for mercy like you made them."

Jedrek kicks Laska in the ribs again.

"For a moment I considered sparing your life. You won't survive this night. I guarantee it."

"If you kill me, my people will come for you."

"I am gonna kill you; nothing you can say will change that."

Jedrek steps on the back of Laska's head smashing his face against the hardwood floor.

"I wonder how much pain can you take before you start begging for mercy? Maybe I'm not trying hard enough. What do you think? What's the matter, cat got your tongue?"

Laska flails his left arm.

"Oh, you can't breathe."

Jedrek removes his foot from Laska's head. Then he bends over and hits Laska in the head with the gun.

"Turn your ass over."

Laska slowly rolls over. He spits out his two front teeth.

"You think you can look me in the eyes when you pull that trigger?"

Jedrek jumps on top of Laska, jamming a knee into his chest. Laska bellows in pain.

"I'm a fair man. I'm gonna give you a chance to make your peace with God before I end you."

"Are you going to talk me to death or are you going to pull that trigger?"

"Ok, have it your way."

Jedrek rests the barrel of the gun on Laska's forehead. Laska stares directly into Jedrek's eyes and begins murmuring something in Russian. Jedrek believes he's cursing. Jedrek smiles and pulls the trigger. The gun clicks. Laska flinches and pees his pants.

"Silly me, I forgot the clip was emptied."

Jedrek sees the pee on the floor.

"Now we're getting somewhere."

"You should go and spend your last moments with your wife. Because you're both dead after this night."

Laska's eyes roll into the back of his head. Jedrek snaps his fingers.

"Hey! Stay with me. It's time for you to die."

Laska looks into Jedrek's eyes again. He's familiar with the look of a killer.

"You don't have to do it," Laska stutters.

"Oh, why not?"

"You've claimed vengeance in her honor. You've proven your manhood."

"But I have to kill you, so you'll never bother her again."

"I won't bother her, I promise. I take back what I said about killing the both of you."

"Yeah right. You don't have the slightest bit of remorse for anything you've done. Even at this very moment, you're probably thinking of ways you can kill me."

"I swear to you I will not harm your wife. I will not seek retribution."

"I know you won't harm her. Because you're gonna be too busy burning in hell."

Jedrek hits Laska in the face with the gun.

Chapter 28

Raisa returns to the house and finds Jedrek standing over Laska's limp body.

"Jeed, what did you do?"

"Raisa, get out, you don't need to see this."

Raisa steps forward.

"Is he dead?"

"I believe so."

Raisa slowly walks over to Jedrek. He rushes to cut her off; standing in front of her to shield her from the gruesome spectacle.

"Don't look."

"I want to see. I need to see."

"No baby, this will give you nightmares," Jedrek says with both arms extended.

"I need to see that he's dead, so the nightmares will stop," she explains trying to peer around him.

Jedrek hesitantly moves aside. Raisa looks down and covers her mouth.

"I told you."

Raisa looks at Jedrek in amazement.

"Don't be afraid; you know I would never hurt you."

She hugs him.

"Hold up, I don't wanna get any blood on your clothes."

"I don't care about that," she says squeezing him tighter.

Jedrek lifts her off the floor.

I was hoping I'd see you again," she sobs.

"I wouldn't have given up until I found you."

"Hey you guys, someone's coming!" Ashley says rushing through the door.

"It might be his crew. You two go hide and no matter what you hear, don't come out until they're gone," Jedrek says.

"I'm not going anywhere," Raisa says.

"If they find you here, they will kill you too."

"If we die, we die together," she grabs his arm.

They hear the noise of car doors slamming simultaneously.

"Go," Jedrek says pointing down the hall.

"Come on," Ashley encourages.

"Go hide," Raisa tells her.

Ashley gives Raisa the gun. Then she takes off down the long hallway. The sounds of footsteps are closing in. Jedrek takes the gun from Raisa.

"Go Raisa," he says with a whisper.

"No."

"And you call me stubborn. Get behind me."

He points the gun at the door. Rafiq walks in.

"Nice to see you too Jed."

Jedrek lowers the gun and lets out a deep breath.

"Jeed, I saw this man earlier. He helped me. How do you know him?"

"Should you tell her, or should I?" Rafiq asks with a smile.

"There's no time for that," Jedrek steps aside revealing Laska's body.

"Damn! You messed him up. You and that damn temper of yours. Burn check this out."

"We have to go," Jedrek says leading Raisa to the door.

"Damn!" I gotta get a closer look at this," Burn says patting Jedrek on the back.

"I'm glad to see y'all are ok," Rafiq says.

"Thank you for helping my wife."

"No doubt," Rafiq responds.

"Thank you," Raisa says.

"You're welcome," Rafiq smiles.

"I hate to cut it short, but we need to get outta here," Jedrek says.

"Wait Jeed, we are forgetting Ashley," Raisa runs down the hall.

"I'll take care of that for you," Rafiq points at the gun in Jedrek's hand.

"Please take it, and while you're at it, you can take this one too."

Jedrek reaches into his pocket and pulls out the empty bloody gun.

"Is this what I think it is?" Rafiq asks.

"I don't ever want to see that thing again."

"I'm dying to know, where you hid it."

"Twenty-first precinct; loose brick in the alleyway side foundation."

Rafiq laughs.

"You said to hide it someplace no one would think to look."

Raisa returns with Ashley. Ashley clutches Raisa's arm tight at the sight of Burn and Rafiq.

"That's our cue," Jedrek says.

"You go ahead. Burn and I are gonna stick around to make sure y'all didn't leave any tracks."

"Thank you."

"Don't mention it. Brothers look out for one another. Even if they don't always see eye to eye."

Jedrek is astonished, unsure how to receive Rafiq's kindness.

"I'll see you around Jed."

"All right."

They bump fists as a show of respect. Jedrek drapes his arm around Raisa's shoulders. Ashley maintains her grip on Raisa's arm as they walk past Rafiq.

"Why did that man call you brother?" Raisa asks Jedrek.

"It's a complicated story."

"I want to hear all about it."

"I'll tell you everything once we put some distance between us and this house," he opens the car doors for Raisa and Ashley.

Rafiq watches them leave; making certain no one bothers them.

"Yo Ra, I'ma take this fool Rolex, you want his pinky ring?" Burn asks.

"Burn, I don't take things from the dead. On second thought, grab his jewelry and anything else of value. We can make this look like a robbery."

Chapter 29

Jedrek suggested Raisa and Ashley see a doctor after their ordeal. He tried not to imagine the atrocities they suffered at the hands of Laska and his men. He dared not ask. Raisa and Ashley both refused to go to the hospital. Raisa told Jedrek and Ashley how Rafiq helped her. It gave Jedrek much comfort.

"Can you give Ashley your phone? She needs to call her parents," Raisa says.

"Sure," Jedrek says reaching into his pocket.

Jedrek hands the phone to Raisa.

"Here Ashley, call your parents. I know they must be worried sick."

Ashley leans forward from the back seat.

"Thank you," she says grabbing the phone.

"You're welcome."

Raisa looks down at her left hand, where her wedding band was.

"With all the excitement I completely forgot, Jedrek says."

He reaches into his pocket and places the ring in her palm.

"My wedding band, but how?"

"I saw it on the floor when I was beating that mother..."

Raisa wipes the ring off with her shirt.

"There was a time when I thought I wouldn't see it or you ever again. Thank you."

"You're safe now."

She nods her head as tears begin to roll down her cheeks.

"There's something else I need to tell you."

"We don't have to talk about this now."

"I've kept this secret far too long. Tonight I watched helplessly as that secret threatened to destroy my love. I cannot go another day without telling you the truth. You deserve to know."

"Then tell me and let me help shoulder your burden."

Raisa smiles at Jedrek.

"I was born Raisa Fedorova, not Raisa Ivanova. I didn't come to this country as a refuge. I was brought here as a sex slave. To be sold off to the highest bidder. The man you killed went by the name Laska.

"He was my captor, a high-ranking soldier in the Russian Mafia. He tricked me. He promised he would help launch my singing career. My father didn't trust him. He tried to warn me, but I was naïve."

"Excuse me, baby. Hey Ashley, tell your dad not to call the police. We don't know who we can trust," Jedrek says.

"Yes, dad I'm fine. I'm with the nice couple that rescued me. And dad, don't call the police. It's a long story but they can't be trusted. Hold on, dad. He says he won't call the police, but he wants to know where you're taking me," Ashley explains.

"120 East Edward Avenue," Jedrek says.

"120 East Edward Avenue, dad. I'm in Tea Town. Yeah, way out here," Ashley continues.

"I'm sorry for cutting across you baby, please continue," Jedrek says to Raisa.

"It's ok. Where was I? Oh yes, how I came to America. I met Laska after I performed in a local talent show. I came in second place. My outfit wasn't as revealing as the winner's. Laska told me he thought I should have won. He told me I didn't need that little competition.

"He told me I could be a star and he could help me. I foolishly believed him to the point I argued with my parents over it. My father said he could smell the evil on Laska. But he was a smooth talker; told me all about his travels across the world.

"He told me about America. I have always wanted to come to America. Ever since I heard 'No More Games,' by Calena Marie. I knew I wanted to be a singer. I dreamed about performing on stage with Calena.

"So, when Laska offered me a plane ticket, I jumped at the opportunity. He said he was doing me a favor and there were no strings attached. I believed him. I should have been alarmed when he told me not to tell my parents about the trip.

"He assured me that I could call them once we arrived in America. I was beginning to have second thoughts but by then it was too late. If only I'd told someone where I was going that day. I was gagged and tied up at gunpoint.

"I was taken to a shipyard and thrown in a metal storage container with eight other girls. We went days without food or water. By the time we landed we were starved and dehydrated; too weak to fight. One of the girls perished during the voyage.

"She was young, no older than 16. Death was a kindness compared to a life of slavery. They took the girl's body God knows where. Probably discarded it like trash. We were taken to a house like the one we just left.

"We were finally fed and given water. Then we were forced to bathe in front of the men. Those pigs thought it was funny. They laughed and jeered at our fear. We were not allowed to dress after the bath. A doctor was brought in to examine us.

"I'll never forget his cold disgusting hands on my body. He informed Laska I was a virgin. Laska grinned with exceeding gladness. I was given some clothes, taken to a separate room, and locked in a cage. I could hear the other girls screaming.

148

"They abused those poor girls. Before I left the room, I heard one of the men say, 'initiation time.' I wondered if I was next. I was all alone in that dark room, even long after the screaming ceased. Then the door opened.

"I was afraid it was my time for initiation. When the light switched on, I saw a woman standing in the doorway. She said she was sent to check on me. Do not be afraid. 'I am Galina, what is your name?' She asked. I told her my name.

"She commented on how beautiful I was. She told me I was one of the lucky ones. Virgins are prized above all for their rarity. I was to be sold on something called, the dark web. It made me cry. She tried to console me by telling me, it wouldn't be so bad.

"The other girls were going to be sold to anyone with a few dollars. I would be sold to a wealthy man and maybe treated like royalty. But only if I obeyed his commands. You'll get a taste of the good life. Surely that is better than your life in poor old Russia, she said.

"All I wanted was to sing. At that moment all I wanted was to see my family again. I asked if she could help me. She said she was sorry, but she couldn't. She didn't have a choice and neither did I. 'It's a shame you have to be sold,' she said.

"If you do as you're told, you'll be fine she said. I cautioned her I would not be a slave, I would escape. Galina looked at the door and then whispered to me. If you do escape, go to Rada's Bistro in the city. Rada is family. She will help you if you make it there. Then she left the room.

"The next morning Laska came in with some lingerie and a camera. He opened the cage and handed me the lingerie. 'Put it on,' he said. I said no and he punched me in the stomach. I fell to my knees. Pick it up and put it on he demanded.

"I did as I was told. He took pictures of me with the lingerie and without. He grabbed me and pulled me in close. He told me it was a shame I was a virgin. We could've had some real fun, but business before pleasure.

"He threw me to the floor, locked the cage, and left me alone. Galina came in with food shortly after. I couldn't even look at her. 'You have to eat something,' she said. I was too worried to eat. I asked her to leave me alone.

"She said it would all be over soon. She left the tray of food and walked out of the room. Sometime later Laska came back. He said he uploaded my pictures to an online auction on the dark web. He wasn't surprised there was a huge interest in me.

"The highest bid at that time was $300,000. He said he wanted to see if I was worth that much. He told me to get on my knees. When I refused, he grabbed me by the neck and forced me to the floor. 'You will learn,' he said.

"He stood over me, unzipped his pants, and exposed himself. He told me to wax it. I warned him, that he'd lose it if he tried to put it in my mouth. He laughed and told me he would hurt me worse if I didn't follow his commands.

"Then he grabbed me by my hair and tried to force me. God was looking out for me. A notification on his phone made him pause. His face lit up when he saw it. 'The bid is now half a million dollars,' he said.

"He patted me on the head like a dog. 'You sweet, good girl, you're going to make me a nice little bit of money. We must celebrate,' he added. He zipped his pants and then helped me up. 'Come, I will see you to a proper bath and a change of clothes.' He put his arm around me and took me out of the cage.

Chapter 30

"Galina prepared a bath for me, whilst a man stood guard outside the bathroom. She thought giving me a rose petal bath would loosen me up, but I ignored her. She mentioned the auction would be over soon. She felt bad because she would never see me again.

"That made me break my silence. I asked again for her help. She said she would get into trouble if she helped. By that time Laska came in rushing Galina; telling her to hurry up and ready me. 'Don't talk to me like that,' she warned him.

"He chuckled. 'Her clothes are on the bed,' he said. Galina handed me a bathrobe and ushered me into the bedroom. Laska said he had good news and bad news for me. The good news is you were sold for $860,000.

"The bad news is you were sold to a sloppy and unpleasant Greek with poor hygiene. 'How could you?' Galina questioned. 'It's just business Galina,' he said. I didn't know what to do. I was too afraid to run and too afraid to stay.

"He made me go with him to a party. He claimed he didn't want to let me out of his sight. I think he wanted me to see it. He wanted me to see what the other girls were forced to do. He was a sick individual. He made me watch.

"The horrors which those girls are forced to endure; I couldn't imagine. Galina was there too. She told me she wouldn't let anyone touch me. Her words gave me a false sense of security. Until her words proved true.

"There was a fight in one of the other rooms. Laska went to go see about it. During the ruckus, Galina hit Laska's thug with a lamp and told me to run. I ran and I didn't look back. Galina, I don't know what happened to her. She saved me. If it weren't for her, I wouldn't be here today."

"What happened after you left the hotel?" Jedrek asks.

"How did you know the party was at a hotel? I didn't tell you where the party was."

"Um."

"How did you know where the party was, Jedrek?"

Jedrek looks at Raisa with a shameful look.

"You were there weren't you?"

"Yes, I was there."

"Please tell me you were not one of the gangsters involved."

"I wasn't with the gang, and I swear I wasn't one of the guys abusing the women."

"Then what were you doing there?"

"I was hanging out with Ra that night. He said we were going to a party. He made it sound sweet so, I went. At one time I'd thought about joining that gang."

"I'm glad you changed your mind."

"I remember how my grandmother worked hard to keep me outta trouble. She would roll over in her grave if I did something that stupid. I realized too late I didn't belong there. I lost my temper when I saw J.R. beating one of those girls.

"It gave me flashbacks of my mother. She was killed by an abusive boyfriend. I hate it when guys beat women. I didn't care that J.R. was the gang leader. I beat him down for what he did to that girl."

"You started the fight?"

"Yes."

"If you already knew about me, why didn't you say anything?"

"You had been through a traumatic experience. I figured you would tell me about it when you were ready. And if you never wanted to talk about it; I could understand why you would choose to forget."

"Yes, I see. Did you get that scar on your face during the fight?"

"No, I got this scar in jail."

"Jedrek, you lied to me! You told me you were never in prison."

"I wasn't in prison. I was in jail, they're two completely different things."

"Don't insult my intelligence. There is no difference. You couldn't come and go as you please in jail, therefore it's a prison."

"You're right, I'm sorry."

"Why did you lie?"

"I lied to you because I didn't think I'd have a chance with you if you knew the truth."

"What were you in prison for?"

"You might find this hard to believe but I was locked up because I wouldn't snitch on a friend."

"Snitch?"

"Tattle."

"Oh."

"I was protecting a friend that protected me."

"Ra?"

"Yeah."

"How long were you in prison?"

"A few weeks."

"What did Ra do that was so bad?"

"I'd rather not say."

"You said, you would tell me everything."

"I promise I will, but not while she's around," Jedrek says pointing in the back seat at Ashley.

Raisa sits back in her chair and folds her arms.

Chapter 31

Jedrek circled the block to make sure they weren't followed. The car behind them turned down the street adjacent to theirs. Jedrek loops around and pulls over to park in front of townhouse 120. He gets out of the car first to make sure it's safe. He gives Raisa and Ashley a head nod after carefully surveying the area.

"Here's your phone Mr. Jeed," Ashley says handing Jedrek the phone.

Jedrek looks at the phone.

"I'm sorry it died on me. My father didn't want to get off the phone."

"No worries," Jedrek says with a smile.

"I'm kinda glad it died. I love my dad, but I was tired of being on the phone."

"You plan on staying outside all night?" Raisa asks while walking to the house.

"What's wrong with her?" Ashley asks Jedrek.

"She's upset with me," Jedrek explains.

"What were you two talking about?"

"The less you know the better."

"Right."

Raisa looks back at Jedrek, then turns to the door. She grabs the knob and is surprised to find the door open.

"Did you leave the door open?" Raisa asks.

"I couldn't have," Jedrek says.

"Do you think someone is in there?" She steps back.

"I'll go in and check."

"Be careful."

Jedrek walks in and flips the light switch. He doesn't see anyone, but he hears a noise coming from the den. It sounds like the tv. He slowly walks to the end of the hall. Raisa and Ashley step inside. Jedrek shushes them.

"What is it?" Raisa whispers.

"I think someone is in there," he mouths.

Raisa scurries to the kitchen and grabs a knife. She tries to give Jedrek the knife.

"What am I gonna do with that if he has a gun?"

Raisa shrugs her shoulders. Jedrek takes the knife, hoping he won't have to find out. He creeps over to the den. Raisa follows and Ashley hides in the kitchen. Jedrek stops just shy of the den's threshold.

"Whatever happens I love you," he whispers in her ear.

"I love you too," she kisses him on the lips.

The door diagonal to the den swings open catching Raisa and Jedrek by surprise. Jedrek quickly spins around, whisking Raisa behind him with one hand, and pointing the knife with the other. The would-be intruder takes a step out of the bathroom. Jedrek springs into action; thrusting the knife forward. Mya screams. Jedrek stops one-third of an inch from Mya's eye.

"Jed it's me, Mya."

"Mya, what the heck are you doing here?" He asks, putting the knife away.

"I was worried," she responds.

Mya looks at Raisa.

"Oh honey, I'm so glad you're safe," Mya says hugging Raisa.

"Thank you for all your help," Raisa says.

"You're welcome. That creep didn't hurt you, did he?" Mya asks, looking Raisa over.

"No, I'm fine."

Mya tries not to stare at Jedrek's bloody clothes.

"You've been sitting here the whole time?" Jedrek asks.

"You left in such a rush. What was I supposed to do? It's not like you gave me any instructions. I didn't know if you'd need my help or not," Mya says.

"I don't mean to sound ungrateful, but we got nervous when we saw the door open."

"Like I said you left in a rush. I didn't know the door was open or I would've closed it."

Jedrek smirks in embarrassment.

"So, is everything ok? Those guys won't be bothering you anymore, will they?"

Mya gathers from their silence, it's best not to ask any more questions.

"I'll call Jasmine and let her know she can stop the search. Raisa's home safe and sound," Mya says breaking the silence.

"Thank you, Mya. And tell Jasmine I said, thanks for looking out too," Jedrek says.

"Will do. Well, I'll be going now. I'm glad to see y'all are all right."

Raisa hugs Mya.

"Thank you again," she says.

"I had to make it up to you. We got off on the wrong foot yesterday. I'm so sorry about that. You're welcome to come by the salon anytime you want."

"I'd like that," Raisa says.

"Good, I'll be seeing you girl. Bye Jed."

"Bye Mya," Jedrek says.

Mya exits.

"I'll go and make sure Ashley is comfortable. Then you and I will talk," Raisa says poking Jedrek in the stomach.

Chapter 32

"There's nothing more relaxing than a nice hot shower after a long day," says Raisa drying her hair with a towel.

Jedrek smiles at Raisa wearing the black bathrobe he bought her.

"How's Ashley?" He asks.

"She's asleep. Poor girl, I don't think she's slept in a while. She ate and passed right out."

Jedrek grabs her hand, staring into her eyes.

"I love you. I'm sorry I lied to you."

"What else have you lied to me about?"

"That was the only lie I ever told you."

"It's a whopper of a lie."

"I never lied about how I feel about you. I know that doesn't justify the lie I told you."

"No, it doesn't. I've been keeping my shameful secret for a while. I was too nervous to tell you about it. I thought that you would treat me differently. Now I find out that you already knew about it. And your past is no more laudable than my own."

"Look at you, using proper words now."

"Shut up," Raisa smiles.

"I'm sorry for breaking your trust. I'll do whatever it takes to earn it back."

"I don't know what I feel right now. Before today, I couldn't imagine you hurting someone."

"Well, I couldn't imagine living without you."

"It's not that you killed Laska that vexes me, but how you killed him. The fact that you don't seem bothered by it. I'm scared to ask, have you killed someone before?"

"Yes."

"Oh my God, who did you kill?"

"It was a guy in jail. It was self-defense I swear."

"I believe you."

"That place was a jungle. You can't show weakness in a place like that. A man tried to kill me," Jedrek says pointing at the scar on his face.

"Why?"

"It was because I witnessed him murder someone else. I was in the wrong place at the wrong time."

"No, why were you there in the first place?"

"After the fight, J.R. wanted me dead. He told Rafiq to kill me himself. He brought an outsider to the party. I was his mess to clean up. If he didn't do it, he'd be ousted from the gang.

"If he was given a choice, why didn't he walk away?"

"Being ousted from a gang isn't a way out, it's more like a death sentence. Not only would he have been targeted by his own gang but by other gangs as well. Rafiq's loyalty was being tested."

Jedrek pauses.

"Then what happened?"

"Rafiq killed J.R. instead. He said J.R. was gonna kill both of us if he didn't. When he came to me and told me what happened he was hysterical. He had never killed anybody before that day.

"He didn't know what to do. I knew it was wrong to help him. But I couldn't turn my back on him. We were like brothers. And he killed a man to protect me. I took the gun and promised him I'd get rid of it."

"Was that the same gun you had earlier?"

"Yes."

Raisa lays her head on Jedrek's shoulder. He puts his arm around her.

"Go on," she says.

"The police brought me in for questioning. They said they had an anonymous tip about my fight with J.R. They probably had an informant at the party. They wanted me to confess or snitch on someone to save myself. I didn't, so they locked me up for as long as they could hold me.

"Without a weapon or a witness to the crime, they had to release me. I was done with Rafiq after that. I shouldn't have been there that night. My grandmother raised me better. She would've been disappointed in me. I was in a bad place when she died. Like I'd lost my will to live."

"You didn't lose your will to live. I think you needed a reason to keep believing; to keep hoping. I think you found it that night at the party. If you'd lost your will, you would've never risked your life to save a woman in duress. I think you lost your way for a moment, but God redeemed you."

"I'd been keeping the pain bottled up. In that moment I let it all loose on J.R."

"You're trying to downplay what you did. You defended that girl because you are a good man. Your grandmother would be proud of you, proud of the man you've become. You were allowed to endure all that to become the man you are, the man I love. Everything happens for a reason."

"You've been through so much and yet you never lose faith."

"Before I knew about Jesus, I would not have thought so. But now I know God makes no mistakes. If you hadn't been there that night, who knows where I'd be. The same God that allowed me to be captured, was the same God that allowed me to escape. He is the same God that kept me safe tonight.

"You never cease to amaze me. You were taken from your family, and you keep pushing on."

"I have faith I will see them again. Remember what the preacher says, 'if He brings you to it, He will bring you through it.' Perhaps being taken was a punishment for disobeying my father. Perhaps I was meant to be in America to meet my true love. Whatever God's plan is I was meant to be here. Just as you were meant to be at the party that night. We are forever intertwined."

"Do you still dream of becoming a professional singer?"

"I don't know anymore. I don't know what God has in store for me. It's not something I pray for."

"Now I know why you don't like listening to music. It reminds you of the past, and what you lost."

"Yes, you know me better than anyone."

"I think we should plan a trip to visit your family."

"Really?"

"Yeah."

She hugs him.

"When do we leave?"

"As soon as we make the arrangements."

"Oh Jeed, I'm so blessed to have you."

"Do you think your family will like me?"

"They will love you!"

"There's only one condition."

"What is it?"

"Will you sing for me one day?"

"Yes," she smiles.

"You're right, my grandmother would be proud of me. For marrying such an amazing woman."

Chapter 33

Earlier today

"This is how you found him?"

"Yes," Klavdii says with a trembling voice.

"Where were you when this was happening?"

"Laska told me to make sure the girls were taken care of."

"So, you were getting your rocks off while Laska was being murdered?"

"No, it wasn't like that."

"Then tell me Klavdii, what was it like? I can't ask Laska what happened to him, he's dead. There's not much use for a bodyguard without a body to guard is there, Klavdii?"

"Please Kazimir, have mercy."

"Who gave you permission to speak my name? Do you believe we are on equal par?"

"No sir! I'm sorry sir!"

"Relax Klavdii, I will not kill you yet. You're going to recall everything about last night first. Get him out of my sight."

Two men step forward and grab Klavdii.

"Make it hurt, and don't stop until he's told you something of importance.

"No! No! I beg you! Klavdii shouts as the two men drag him off.

"It looks like a robbery gone bad," says a man wearing an eyepatch.

"Whatever gave you that idea?" Kazimir asks.

"Some of his things are missing, like his pinky ring. That was his father's ring. He would have parted with his life before giving up that ring."

"No, my old comrade I don't believe this was a robbery. Look at his condition. Do you think a thief would waste time beating a man to death, just to steal his goods? Even the most inexperienced thieves would know. You only have a few seconds to get in and get out.

"He's been mutilated, no knack whatsoever. Someone took their time here. This wasn't business, it was personal. Then they stole his jewelry to throw us off. A $150,000 car sitting in the driveway with the key still in the ignition. And was there something in the trunk?"

"About 20 grand," another man says.

"I don't think a thief would leave that behind. Someone came here to settle the score. Laska crossed a lot of people. The question is, which one came back for revenge?" Kazimir asks.

"Perhaps it was the Black Gate Boys that did this. Laska had a meeting with them last night," the man with the eyepatch says.

"Rafiq is crazy enough to kill Laska, but he'd be smart enough to kill me first. Call Alik, tell him to get his ass over here now," Kazimir says.

"I tried to call him sir," a man replies.

"Well call him again! I want some answers and I want them now. Wake the neighbors. Someone knows something, or we will tear this neighborhood apart until we find someone that does."

The man nods his head in agreement and walks out with the phone to his ear.

"Whoever did this to you will pay; that I promise," Kazimir says looking upon Laska.

Chapter 34

Rafiq is awakened by the constant pounding on his front door.

"What the hell? That better not be a Jehovah's Witness knocking on my door this early."

Rafiq angrily gets out of bed.

"Who is it?" He stumbles down the dark hallway.

"Yo Ra it's me," Burn says.

"Burn?!" You, banging on my door like you the police," Rafiq snatches the door open.

"My bad Ra, he said it was urgent."

Burn stands in between Kazimir and one of his bodyguards.

"I would like to have a word with you," Kazimir says.

"It must be important if you stopped by this early," Rafiq responds.

"When I show my face, you should know it is very important."

"Come on in," Rafiq ushers.

Kazimir enters. His brutish bodyguard donning an eyepatch over his left eye tries to follow.

"You wait here," Rafiq says blocking the doorway.

"I'll keep an eye on him," Burn says.

The man gives Burn a mean look.

"No offense Mr. Cyclops," Burn says with a grin.

Rafiq closes the door. He takes Kazimir to his office. Kazimir takes a seat in the chair adjacent to Rafiq's desk.

"Now what's so important it couldn't wait?" Rafiq asks.

"A Russian is dead."

"My condolences."

"Thank you."

"Now what does that have to do with me?"

"You should know that Russian was my nephew, Laska. Someone killed him."

"No surprise there, the guy was a prick. I'm sure a lot of people wanted him dead."

"I like you, Rafiq. You have always been the type of guy to tell it like it is. But tread carefully when talking about the dearly departed in my presence."

"What do you expect me to say? I didn't care for your nephew, but I didn't kill him. I thought about it several times though."

"I didn't think you would. We've had a profitable business association. Why would you want to ruin that?"

"Then why are you here?"

"This took place near your territory, and I am searching for answers."

"I don't have any for you."

"I want you and your gang to get out there and get me some answers."

"We don't work for you."

"My generosity knows no bounds. A great reward awaits the person who provides me with the information I seek."

"That's not what we do. Black Gate Boys aren't snitches for hire. You should leave now."

"I will hunt down the person responsible and if I find them in your neighborhood, you'll be sorry."

"Are you threatening me? 'Cause you know I don't respond too well to threats."

"I know you very well, Rafiq the weed peddler. A man who thinks he's too good to sell china and snow in his neighborhood. But not too good to allow others to sell it to his people for a small percentage. You believe your conscience is clear.

"That you are doing something noble. You, aid in your people's extinction, even line them up for me. You do not want to be seen as a villain as if you love your neighborhood.

"The same Rafiq that is pointing a gun at me under his desk right now. Go ahead and pull the trigger.

Snuff me like you did J.R. I know all about you Rafiq. I know everything."

"Except who killed Laska."

"Touché Rafiq, that is an oversight I will soon correct. You can uncock that gun now. I will see myself out."

Kazimir leaves the house. Burn rushes in.

"So, I guess the cat's outta the bag?" Burn asks.

"Yeah, I expected he would react that way. I don't think he's buying the whole robbery ploy."

"I told you that wouldn't work."

"What did you do with Laska's jewelry?"

"Don't worry, I put it in a safe place. What's our next move?"

"I gotta warn Jed."

"Is that wise?"

"Jed and his wife won't be safe here. Kazimir is out for blood, and he won't stop until he gets it. They should leave town before Kazimir figures it out."

"Suppose Kazimir is only playing you? He might suspect we know something about Laska. He may use you to lure Jed into a trap. He's clever like that."

"If I act too fast it could have consequences. If I act too slow it could have consequences also. I can't just sit here and do nothing."

Chapter 35

"I didn't think Ashley and her dad would ever leave," Jedrek says to Raisa.

"He was just excited to have his daughter back."

"Look I'm happy for the guy; now they can go celebrate at their house."

"He's especially grateful for what you did to Laska. Speaking of which, do you think it was wise to tell him you killed Laska?"

"I felt he should know the man who kidnapped his daughter is no longer a threat to anyone. I would wanna know if I were in his shoes."

"Yeah, but suppose he tells someone?"

"If I didn't tell him Ashley would've. That girl will probably need therapy after all this."

"She'll be ok, I was."

"I hope she's as strong as you," Jedrek hugs her.

She smiles.

"I'm going back to bed, you coming?"

Raisa shakes her head no.

"Why not?"

"I have to get started on breakfast."

"Breakfast? I know you're not going to work today? You barely had any sleep."

"I'm starting a new job today. I want to make a good first impression on my new boss."

"I'm not your boss. I'm your partner."

"Say it again."

"I'm your partner."

She kisses him on the lips.

"Again."

"I'm your partner."

"I love you," she says kissing him.

"I love you too."

"Stay up and watch the sunrise with me. It will be like on our first date."

"Sure, after that I'm going to bed."

She pulls him closer to the living room. The doorbell chimes.

"Now who is that this early in the morning?"

"Probably Ashley and Mr. Rodriguez," Raisa says walking to the door.

"I hope not," Jedrek says walking behind her.

Raisa looks through the peephole.

"It's for you," she steps aside.

"For me?"

Jedrek opens the door.

"Ra, what are you doing here?"

"Can I come in?" Rafiq asks.

"Do you have any drugs or weapons on you?"

"I don't have any drugs on me, but you already know I don't leave home without my gun."

"Come on in," Raisa says.

"What are you doing?" Jedrek asks.

"Be nice, he's our guest," she says.

"We're cool and all but that doesn't change the fact that he's a criminal. Whatever he's got going on, I don't want that around you. I don't want any part of it," Jedrek tells Raisa.

"I didn't come here to start trouble. I came here to tell you something," Rafiq explains.

"You can start by telling me how you know where we live."

"Do you really want me to explain that?"

Jedrek gives Rafiq a serious look.

"Okay, to be honest, I followed you home the other day. I wanted to make sure no one messed with you."

"Like who, your gang? Why would they wanna mess with me?"

"I think some of the guys want revenge for J.R. They're just biding their time for the right moment. I didn't want you to get caught in the middle of it."

"Well, thanks for the concern."

"No thanks necessary, we're family."

"Family? Is that what we are? It's hard to tell after you visited the shop yesterday."

"I was wrong for that and I'm sorry. I know I'm not welcome here. I tried to call you to avoid coming over here. But what I have to tell you is very important."

"He is your brother Jeed. He protected you, just like he protected me last night. You don't have to agree with his lifestyle, but don't give up on him," Raisa says.

Rafiq smiles at her.

"What is it you have to tell me Ra?"

"Kazimir came to see me and he's looking for answers."

"Who? Answers about what?"

"Destroyer of Peace," Raisa says.

"How did you know that?" Rafiq asks.

"That's what his name means in Russian," she responds.

"He's the head of the Russian mafia. He wants answers for the death of his nephew Laska," Rafiq explains.

"After everything that happened; now this. I thought there'd be repercussions, but I was hoping," Jedrek says.

"I tried to stop you from going to Laska's house. You and that temper of yours," Rafiq says.

"What am I up against?"

"A man that can kill you by snapping his fingers."

"Maybe I can appeal to him. Let him know his nephew came after my wife. That I killed him to stop him from hurting her."

"It won't matter with him. Laska was his blood. Your best bet is to leave town."

"And go where?"

"As far away from here as you can possibly go."

"I've heard stories about Kazimir. I heard he once killed a man and his entire family because he thought the man was conspiring against him. Rafiq is right we must leave."

"Yeah, but for how long?" Jedrek asks.

"You may never be able to return," Rafiq says.

"Why are we talking like he already knows?"

"And suppose he figures it out; that's a risk you can't afford to take."

"This is a lot to take in," Jedrek says.

"We should take a break from such heavy thoughts. I'll prepare breakfast and then we can discuss our plans. Rafiq, would you care to join us?"

"I could eat," Rafiq says with a grin.

Chapter 36

Klavdii writhes in agony, the result of being hit several times with a baseball bat. Kazimir walks in clapping.

"You have proven you can take a beating, but your life is worth little to me right now. Yet you still have a chance to redeem yourself. Tell me something of importance," Kazimir demands.

"I told them everything I remember," Klavdii says.

"Help him refresh his memory," Kazimir tells the man holding the bat.

The man hits Klavdii again and again. A man wearing a gray suit walks in.

"Did your labor bear fruit?" Kazimir asks.

"Yes sir," the man responds.

"And what did you find out?"

"The pervert down the road from Laska said, a teenage girl wandered into his yard. A Mexican girl."

Kazimir turns to Klavdii.

"Now that is interesting. Continue."

"He said, Laska caught the girl and took her back to his place," the man adds.

"And what time was that?" Kazimir asks.

"Before midnight."

"What do you know of this girl?" Kazimir asks Klavdii.

"She was a hitchhiker we picked up," Klavdii answers.

"A foolish thing to pick up a hitchhiker, you risk being caught that way."

"He said he was taking her back to his place to have some fun with her."

"Do you think a little girl killed Laska?" Kazimir scoffs.

"They didn't look tough, but they put up a fight."

"They? So, someone else was there? Who was it?"

"There was another girl."

"Tell me about her."

"It was the girl from Rada's Bistro."

"Which one?"

"The beautiful one, with curly hair."

"You mean Raisa," the man with the eyepatch says.

"I know of her. Why was she with Laska? And don't lie to me," Kazimir says.

"Laska heard, the girl had been talking too much about things she shouldn't have."

"Who told him that?"

"He never said."

"How convenient. Then what happened?"

"Laska and I went to pay her a visit."

"Without my authorization."

"He just wanted to scare her. When she raised a ruckus, we took her. It was on the spur of the moment."

"That makes no sense. The girl stayed quiet for so long. Then Laska winds up dead shortly after he returns to Tea Town. Are you sure he didn't bring this on himself?"

Klavdii shakes his head no.

"That still doesn't explain what happened to Laska. I fail to believe that petite girl could've done him in," Kazimir says.

"Maybe it was her husband," Klavdii suggests.

"The black man. What is his name?" Kazimir asks.

"Jedrek," someone answers.

"He's a mechanic. He does good work and he's affordable," another man adds.

"One of ours is dead and you're advertising for the man's business. This is no time for a damn commercial break," Kazimir says.

"Sorry sir," the man says.

"I need to know the nature of the man. If he is capable of murder," Kazimir declares.

"Raisa's beauty would drive any man to kill," a man says.

"It's a shame, that beautiful girl married a wog, Kazimir says."

"You mean to tell me you've never been with a black woman?" Asks the man with the eyepatch.

"I've had a few black beauties in my day," Kazimir smirks.

They all laugh, including Klavdii.

"Who told you, you could laugh?" Kazimir asks.

Klavdii stops laughing. Kazimir reaches into his pocket and pulls out a knife. He presses the blade against Klavdii's throat.

"Please," Klavdii begs.

Kazimir cuts the rope unbinding him from the chair.

"You get to keep your life, for now. If you're lying to me, you'll receive far worse. Go get cleaned up."

A man escorts Klavdii out.

"Keep an eye on him," Kazimir orders the man.

"Sir, if I may? Allow me to bring the black mechanic to you," a man with blond hair says.

"Young Vasily, you're showing such initiative. It would be an insult not to honor your request. Go, bring me the mechanic and his wife."

Chapter 37

"Would you like some more?" Raisa asks.

"No thank you, Mrs. Mann," Rafiq says.

"Please, call me Raisa."

"Well Raisa, the food was great. I couldn't eat another bite. Where'd you learn to cook like that?"

"My mother taught me."

"I didn't know Russian women could cook like that."

"You should never judge a book by its cover."

They both laugh. Jedrek sits there in deep thought.

"Are you all, right?" Raisa asks Jedrek.

"Huh?" He responds.

"You barely touched your breakfast," she says.

"I'm sorry baby, I'm not hungry."

"I'm not worried about the food. I'm worried about you. What's on your mind?" she grabs his hand.

"I don't wanna leave. This is our home; everything we worked hard for. What's gonna happen to the shop? I finally get you to come work with me, now we have to kiss it goodbye."

Raisa looks at Jedrek with a grim look.

"None of that matters, as long as we're together," she says.

He kisses her hand.

"Sell me the shop," Rafiq suggests.

"I'm not gonna let you ruin the shop with your shady business," Jedrek says.

"It's not like that. I'm trying to give you some money to help you relocate."

"I don't want any of your dirty money."

"My money's not honest, I'll admit that. But I'm making this offer outta love and that's the honest to God truth."

"And you want something in return. Thank you but no thank you. We have some money saved up. We'll get by with that until we can find a buyer."

"How long will your money last? How long will it take till you find a buyer? How will you arrange a sale when you go into hiding?"

Jedrek looks at Raisa.

"What do you think?"

She nods her head yes.

"What choice do we have on such short notice?" She asks.

"Make me an offer," Jedrek says.

"How about 300 thousand?"

"Are you serious?"

"Yes, I'm serious. Do we have a deal?"

"Deal."

"You always keep money stashed away for a rainy day?" Raisa asks.

"Of course, who do you think taught Jedrek how to save money?" Rafiq brags.

"Grandma taught us how to save money," Jedrek says.

"Yes, she did. That woman could pinch a penny. She always kept us clothed and fed, even on the darkest days.

Jedrek nods his head in agreement.

"Don't worry about the shop. I'll leave it the way it is that includes business practices and employees."

"I don't care if you fire Darrell."

They laugh.

"Well, I guess we should start making travel plans," Raisa says grabbing her laptop.

"We appreciate everything," Jedrek says shaking Rafiq's hand.

"Hey man, we're family. We'll always have each other's back."

"I'll probably never be able to repay you."

"You can repay me by living. Whatever you do, don't tell anybody where you're going; not even me. Don't contact anyone, especially by phone. And stay away from familiar areas."

"Such as?"

Places you've vacationed; places you might've mentioned you'd like to visit. I know it's a lot to consider. I'll leave y'all to discuss it. I'll be back shortly with the money."

"I'll get started with transferring ownership. We'll need a notary."

"I got somebody."

Jedrek shows Rafiq to the door. Rafiq's phone vibrates from an incoming call.

"It's probably Burn," Rafiq implies.

"Later then," Jedrek says.

Rafiq looks at his phone. He frowns at the number on the caller ID.

"It's Kazimir," Rafiq says.

"You gonna answer it?"

"Yeah, I'm curious to hear what he has to say. Don't make a sound."

Raisa takes her hands off the keyboard.

"Yeah," Rafiq answers the phone."

"Well, hello to you too. I didn't think you'd answer the phone given our last exchange," Kazimir says.

"If you have something to say, just tell it to me straight," Rafiq says.

"Let me begin by offering my sincerest apologies for our last interaction. News of my nephew's passing has sent me over the edge. But I want you to know there is no animosity between us."

"That's good to hear. To be honest, I didn't give it a second thought, but thanks anyway."

"No, I must commend you. You are a self-made man like me. I acknowledge that it was you who brought peace between the gangs in Tea Town. Something your predecessor would've never attempted. We must break bread someday soon, to discuss future business opportunities."

"Sounds good, so I guess you've given up that wild goose chase you were on?"

"Quite the contrary, I have info towards the matter."

"What kinda info?"

"I have a name."

"Who?"

"A mechanic."

Rafiq's eyes widen.

"Goes by the name of Jedrek. Do you know him?"

"I can't say that I do."

"I believe he's the one I'm seeking. I sent some men to fetch him."

"You did what?" Rafiq asks peeking through the beige Venetian blinds.

"Are you hard of hearing? I sent some men to fetch him."

"Where'd you send them?"

"That is none of your concern. You had a chance to be a part of the search."

"Right."

"I'll be in touch," Kazimir hangs up.

"We gotta get outta here!" Rafiq exclaims.

"What is it?" Raisa asks.

"They're on their way," Rafiq says scrolling through his phone.

Jedrek looks at Raisa.

"Jed we gotta move now!" Rafiq says.

"Baby put your shoes on," Jedrek calmly tells Raisa.

"Jedrek grabs his running shoes next to the door.

"Yo Burn, I need you to come get us asap. Hold on," Rafiq looks out the window.

A black SUV pulls up and four men wearing suits get out.

"Aw crap, they're here. Where's your back door?" Rafiq asks grabbing his gun.

"Through there," Jedrek points.

"Burn we're coming out the back door, meet us one street over."

Rafiq puts his phone back into his pocket. There is a knock on the front door.

"Stay cool," Rafiq whispers as they stop at the back door.

Jedrek holds on tight to Raisa.

"I'll go first," Rafiq says pointing the gun at the door.

Raisa closes her eyes. Rafiq jerks the door open. They're relieved no one is there. The intensity of the knocking increases. They dash through the door, not a second too soon. The front door comes crashing down in the background.

The trio runs through a neighbor's backyard. Jedrek holding onto Raisa's hand tight with Rafiq bringing up the rear; looking over his shoulder. They arrive at the rendezvous point.

"Come on Burn," Rafiq says.

"Where's your car?" Jedrek asks.

"I had Burn drop me off down the road from your house in case somebody followed me. You're welcome."

Jedrek gives Rafiq a humbling look.

"There!" Raisa says pointing at the royal blue 87' Chevy Caprice closing in.

Burn brings the car to a screeching halt.

"Did you forget how to get over here?" Rafiq asks Burn as he gets in the passenger seat.

"It's nice to see you too," Burn retorts.

Jedrek and Raisa hop in the back seat. Then they speed off.

Chapter 38

"Is anyone home? We don't mean you any harm. We only want to talk," Vasily says leading a group of thugs into the house.

The men split up to search the rooms.

"I'm sorry about the door. My friends can be a little overzealous," Vasily continues walking into the bedroom.

He looks under the bed.

"I'm sure there's just a misunderstanding. If you come out maybe, we can sort this out together. What do you say?" Vasily asks opening the closet door.

"There is no one here," says a bald man standing in the doorway.

"Their car is still here, Vasily says."

"Maybe they walked."

"That would be stupid."

"The backdoor was unlocked."

"Take the truck and circle the block then."

Vasily notices Jedrek's car key on the nightstand next to the bed. He grabs the key and walks outside to Jedrek's car. He sees wet spots in the driver's seat, where someone attempted to remove stains. He checks the trunk. Finding a garbage bag with bloody clothes puts a smile on his face.

"It looks like the butler did do it," he says.

Vasily grabs the bag and goes back into the house.

"Did you find anything else?" He asks a man wearing a navy-blue suit.

"Yes, a computer," The man says handing it to him.

Vasily reaches for his phone; he calls Kazimir.

"Do you have him?" Kazimir asks.

"No sir, it looks like we just missed them," Vasily answers.

"Did you find anything?"

"Yes, some bloody clothes and a computer. Looks like someone is planning a trip to St. Croix."

"Go search the airport."

"Yes sir."

"Any word from Alik?"

"No."

"Alik says he's ready to be the boss but once again he proves otherwise. I'm offering a bounty for Jedrek the mechanic. One hundred grand to the one who delivers him to me alive. I'll even settle for half alive."

"And his wife?"

"She's not important," Kazimir says ending the call.

Kazimir calls Rafiq again.

"Yo," Rafiq answers.

"You answered on the first ring; that shows respect. My son Alik could learn a thing or two from you," Kazimir states.

"What's up?" Rafiq asks.

"I want you to help me find Jedrek the mechanic."

"I thought it was none of my concern."

"He gave us the slip."

"Any leads?"

"We suspect he may be headed to the airport. I want him alive. There's a hundred-thousand-dollar price on his head. That should be more than enough to motivate you and your boys to join the search."

"A hundred grand for a mechanic?"

Rafiq peers in the back seat at Jedrek.

"That is tempting but we'll sit this one out. Dog catching ain't our thing," Rafiq explains.

"Suit yourself," Kazimir says.

Rafiq hangs up the phone.

"Thanks," Jedrek says.

"No thanks required. They'll be plenty of lowlifes out to collect Kazimir's bounty," Rafiq declares.

"Did I hear you say he's offering a hundred thousand dollars for us?" Jedrek asks.

"Just you, he wants you alive."

"What about Raisa?"

"He didn't mention her."

Trying not to imagine the worst-case scenario; Jedrek looks her in the eyes.

"Don't worry, I won't let anything happen to you," he says.

"There's more bad news. He has some guys waiting for you at the airport," Rafiq says.

"This is all my fault," Jedrek says.

Raisa hugs him tight.

"Come on Jed this is like old times. Remember snatch and grab at the old Arab store. That old lady used to chase us down the road with a broom."

Jedrek laughs.

"I remember that day she hit you in the head with that broom," Jedrek says.

"Man, that's not funny; that old heifer gave me a concussion."

They all laugh.

"Where are we going?" Jedrek asks.

"To a safe house. No one else knows about it, except me and Burn. Once y'all are safe, I'll go and get the money I promised you."

"Oh crap," Burn says.

"What is it?" Raisa asks.

"Police checkpoint up ahead," Burn explains.

"They probably work for Kazimir," Rafiq says.

"Let's just turn around," Jedrek suggests.

"Too late, they've seen us," Rafiq says.

"Maybe they don't know what Jed looks like," Burn says.

"It's not Jed I'm worried about. Raisa sticks out like a sore thumb."

Hey, miss, duck down to the floor. Here Jed, take this and drape it over your wife," Burn says handing Jedrek his jacket.

Burn slows the car down and inches it forward. The car in front of them is being waved on. The policeman signals Burn to stop.

"I need to see your license," the officer says.

Burn reaches in his back pocket.

"Y'all looking for a fugitive or something?" Burn asks handing the officer a fake ID.

Rafiq looks at Burn.

"Just a routine checkpoint," the officer says looking over the phony license.

"Checking for drunk drivers this early in the morning? Burn asks.

"It's four p.m. somewhere," the officer says passing Burn the ID.

"Can I go now?"

"Now I need to see their IDs."

"What the hell do you need to see my ID for? I ain't driving fool," Rafiq retorts.

"Don't piss me off boy," the officer warns.

"It's better to be pissed off than to be pissed on," Rafiq says.

"What's the hold up over here?" Another officer asks.

"They won't show me their IDs," The first officer says.

"Black Gate Boys, I didn't think you little pissants left your own turf. Where are you headed?" The second officer asks.

"Yo mama's house," Burn responds.

Rafiq laughs.

"Get the hell outta here," The second officer commands.

"Wait a minute, what's that back there on the floor?" The first officer asks.

"We have bigger things to worry about besides them. I doubt they're hiding someone under that coat. Let them go," the second officer whispers.

"Well, you heard him. Get the hell outta here," the first officer says.

"Thank you, I'll tell yo mama you said, hey," Burn says driving away.

"It's safe baby," Jedrek tells Raisa.

"Your friends are crazy," she says.

Jedrek helps her up.

"Was all that necessary?" Jedrek asks.

"We're just being our usual charming selves," Rafiq explains.

"We almost got caught with y'all pissing the cops off like that," Jedrek says.

"If we acted nervous, they would've gotten suspicious," Rafiq says.

"Relax man we got your back," Burn adds.

Chapter 39

The group managed to get to the safe house without any more close calls. Rafiq decided to travel back to the city by himself, leaving Burn behind to protect the couple. Rafiq didn't want to waste time. He finally arrived at his home after being hindered by two more checkpoints. As he hurries up the steps a car pulls up. Rafiq sees its Rell and Hype.

"What do these fools want?" He asks himself.

"Yo Ra!" Rell runs up the steps.

"What up Rell?"

"Word on the street is, everyone's looking for your boy the mechanic."

"Where'd you hear that?"

"Don't worry about it."

"I already told Kazimir we're not touching him."

"Why would you do that?"

"Let me explain this in a way you'll understand. Some people believe there's more to life than money and power. I believe it's wrong to hunt down a brother like a dog and hand him over for a little bit of change."

"A hundred grand Ra."

"I told y'all the other day, he's not to be messed with."

"That was different. You gave him a free pass to walk on our turf. A hundred grand, his pass is revoked."

"It's good as long as I say it's good."

"I think the others will agree with me."

"I said what I said. Make sure you let the others know we're not touching him. You hear me?" Rafiq asks showing his gun.

Rell smirks.

"Now if you'll excuse me. I have some important business to attend to."

"This ain't over."

Rafiq closes the door in his face. Rafiq makes sure they leave his yard before he continues his plan. He goes into his bedroom. Next to his bed lies a Persian rug. Under the rug is a floor safe. The combination is the date of his mother's death.

"Rest in peace ma," he whispers opening the safe.

There's some jewelry and close to $11,000 in cash; a decoy for the real treasure. Underneath the cash is a box with a key. Rafiq takes the key and leaves the room. He goes into the kitchen and grabs a raw steak from the fridge.

Then out the back, cautiously looking around. He grabs a shovel propped against the house. He walks around to the outdoor cellar entrance. A large white pit bull rests in front of the cellar doors. The dog growls at Rafiq.

"Quiet Snowman, it's just me."

Rafiq tosses the raw steak to the dog. The dog catches the steak before it hits the ground.

"Good boy."

The doors are chained together and bound by a heavy-duty padlock. Rafiq uses the key to unlock it. He descends into the cellar with the shovel in hand. About 10 feet from the bottom step rests a crate stamped Blue Dream. Rafiq pushes the crate and digs up the earth floor.

"Pay dirt," he says striking a hard surface with the shovel.

Rafiq uncovers a trunk. He opens the trunk and looks at the stacks of money; over 300 thousand dollars in large bills. Rafiq stuffs the money in a duffle bag and leaves the house.

Chapter 40

By the time Rafiq makes his way back to the safe house. The streets are crawling with all kinds of ungodly souls, seeking to become richer. Rafiq contemplates how to help Jedrek, and Raisa escape the madness. He exercises extreme caution. He must be careful, riding around with a bag full of money.

Rafiq takes the scenic route through town. He imagines he'll encounter less traffic that way. Nothing could've prepared Rafiq for the sight of Jedrek's shop. He stops to get a good look. The windows have been shattered. The inside of the shop appears to have been ransacked.

A message that reads, "you can't hide," is spray-painted on the outer wall. In the parking lot, two of Jedrek's employees talk with the police. Rafiq knows they probably work for Kazimir. He guesses they are questioning the mechanics on their boss's whereabouts and not at all concerned about the vandalism.

"Whoever did this will pay with their lives," Rafiq declares.

He makes up his mind not to tell Jedrek about the shop. It would break his heart. Whatever plan they come up with; they'll have to wait until nightfall to implement it. The streets are too hot and it's too risky to transport the couple in broad daylight. On the other hand, the longer they wait could also prove challenging.

After taking his precautious time, Rafiq finally arrives at the safe house. He pops the trunk and retrieves the duffle bag.

"What up Ra?" Rell asks holding a gun to the back of Rafiq's head.

Hype steps out in front of Rafiq pointing a gun at him.

"I should've known you'd be here too. You can't make any moves without your boyfriend," Rafiq tells Hype.

"I can't believe you let me sneak up on you. You're slipping Ra," Rell says.

"How the hell did y'all find me?" Rafiq asks.

"At a time like this, that's what you wanna know? Rell asks.

"What brings you all the way out here, in the middle of nowhere? What's behind door number one?" Hype asks.

"I know you can't be as stupid as you look, so let's cut the crap. It's over a quarter of a million dollars in this duffle bag. That's more than Kazimir's bounty. Just take the money and go."

"We're gonna take your money anyway. Then we're gonna go in the house and collect that reward," Rell says.

"Forget about what you have planned. It's not worth losing your life over."

"You're not in a position to make threats."

Rafiq quickly spins around, hitting Rell with the duffle bag. Money flies everywhere. Rell drops his gun. Hype squeezes off two shots, catching Rafiq in the back. Rafiq is stopped in his tracks. Rell laughs.

"The Black Gate Boys are under new management," Rell says standing over Rafiq.

Rell aims his gun at Rafiq's face. The front door to the safe house swings open. An enraged Burn wastes no words. Instead, rapid-fire from his gun claims the life of Hype instantly. Rell and Burn set their sights on each other. Burn shoots first but misses.

Rell returns fire, one bullet narrowly missing Burn's head, another one striking his shoulder. Dropping his gun in the doorway, Burn staggers back into the house. Rell rushes up the porch steps. Jedrek reaches for Burn's gun but Rell stomps on his hand.

"Too slow," Rell says.

Jedrek stares down the barrel of Rell's gun.

"Get up…slowly," Rell commands.

Jedrek complies.

"Where's Burn?" Rell asks.

"I don't know," Jedrek says clutching his injured hand.

"Don't play dumb with me. I know he's in here hiding."

"I'm right here punk," Burn says sitting on the floor in the corner.

"There he is. I knew you would never run from a fight," Rell smirks.

"Man, get on with it. I'm tired of hearing your whiny voice," Burn says.

"Apologize to Ra when you see him," Rell says.

"No, don't shoot!" Raisa exclaims.

She enters the room with her hands up.

"What are you doing?" Jedrek asks.

"Well, hello again, I remember you. You're that stuck up hoe from the party," Rell says.

"Don't talk to my wife like that," Jedrek cautions.

"Oh, she's your woman?" Rell asks with a laugh.

"We will go with you if you promise not to kill him," Raisa says.

"You mean Burn?" Rell asks.

"Yes," she replies.

"Well, here's the thing, Kazimir only wants Jedrek. So, I don't need you or, Burn."

Jedrek steps in front of Rell.

"I'm not gonna let you kill my wife."

"Get the hell outta my face," Rell demands.

"You'll have to kill me first," Jedrek says.

"Kazimir said he wants you alive. I guess he'll have to settle for barely alive."

Rell aims the gun at Jedrek's kneecap. The loud sound of a gunshot thunders through the house. Rell topples over from a shot to his spinal cord. Jedrek looks to see Rafiq in the doorway holding a smoking gun. Rell reaches for the gun next to him. Jedrek stomps his hand.

"Too slow," he says.

Burn laughs. Rafiq kneels next to Rell.

"How?" Rell asks.

"At a time like this, that's what you wanna know? You should be wondering why I didn't blow your brains out," Rafiq says.

"You lost your nerve," Rell laughs.

Rafiq reaches into his back pocket.

"I wanted to see the look on your face when I did this."

Rafiq pulls out a knife and stabs Rell in the throat. Raisa cringes from the gory sight. Jedrek watches as the life flees from Rell's body.

"Say hi to J.R. for me," Rafiq says wiping the blade on Rell's pants.

"We thought you were dead," Jedrek says.

Rafiq lifts his shirt.

"Bulletproof vest," Jedrek smiles.

Raisa grabs a towel and applies pressure to Burn's wound.

"We have to get him to a doctor," she says.

"He'll be all right. Burn's been through worse," Rafiq says.

Burn points at the scar on his neck where a bullet almost claimed his life years earlier.

"How's it look?" Rafiq asks.

"The bullet went straight through," Burn responds.

"Good, we'll get you patched up in just a second. First, I gotta get this dead fool outta my house before he stinks up the place."

Rafiq grabs Rell by the feet and drags his body out of the house.

Chapter 41

The group worked together to pick up the pieces. Despite having two possible broken fingers, Jedrek helped Rafiq bury the bodies in the backyard. Raisa bandaged Burn's shoulder and gave him some painkillers.

Burn helped to calm Raisa down by telling her how he got his nickname. It was an amusing story, involving a cigarette lighter exploding in his pocket. Hours have passed and still no plan. Escorting the couple to safety was a longshot. Now with Burn injured it's almost impossible.

"I appreciate everything you've done for us," Jedrek says.

"It's all love," Rafiq says.

"I feel guilty about taking your money."

"Why, because how I got it?"

"That's the main reason. Plus, we never transferred ownership of the shop."

"Not much I can do with the shop now."

"What do you mean?"

Rafiq remains silent about the current state of the shop.

"Don't worry about it. I can always make more dough," Rafiq comments.

"You've always had good intentions. If you let Christ into your heart…"

"Stop right there. I don't need you trying to preach to me right now."

"I'm not trying to preach to you. I'm trying to encourage you."

"Some of us don't have a choice in how we live."

"That's crap and you know it. I grew up in the same projects as you."

"You had it better than I did."

"How? Neither one of us knew our fathers."

"My mom died from a drug overdose."

"My mom was killed by her boyfriend."

"At least you had your grandmother to steer you in the right direction."

"She was there for you too."

"But she wasn't my blood."

"Blood couldn't make us anymore related."

"You don't know what it's like being me. You never got teased for being light-skinned. You never had to worry about people calling you names. I had to fight almost every day to prove myself."

"I remember, we fought side by side. What do you fight for now?"

"I fight to survive, same as before."

"By putting yourself at risk each day. That's a wasted life."

"This is my life. It's like your wife said, you don't have to agree with it."

"Is there a purpose behind all the money, any ambition? Is there nothing else you strive for?"

They eyeball one another. Not wanting to say anything else to upset the other.

"My bad, I'm not judging you," Jedrek says breaking the awkward silence.

"It's all good."

"I'm not mad at you. I have a lot on my mind is all."

"I know you have a lot on your mind right now. Nobody can blame you for being on edge. Just try not to worry. I'll get y'all outta this town or die trying."

"No one else has to die. I know what needs to be done."

"No more thoughts about giving up."

Jedrek gestures to Raisa sleeping on the couch.

"Look at her. It's the most peaceful I've seen her since this all started."

"You're not gonna waltz in there and hand yourself over, are you? What would that solve? They still might come after her."

"Yeah, but if I can distract them long enough for you to get her to safety. It would be worth it. I'm the one he wants, remember?"

"What good are you to her, dead? She would probably kill herself."

"No, she wouldn't. She's stronger than both of us."

"You've been contemplating this since we left your house. And is it part of your plan to leave without saying goodbye to your wife?"

"They were gonna kill her Ra. That man didn't even waver. He was gonna shoot her dead right in front of me."

"And someone still might if they find her. That's why you have to get the hell outta town Jed."

"But Ra there's no place to go. You said this man has connections everywhere and his reach, who knows how far. What kinda life is that? Always having to look over our shoulders, everywhere we go. Never being able to stay in one place for a long time."

"At least you would be together. It wouldn't be a perfect life, but it would be a life. You just need to…"

"Need to what?"

"You need to pray like grandma said."

"I thought you didn't believe in prayer?"

"I believe in God. I just haven't called on Him in a long time. I feel like, maybe He gave up on me."

"God never gives up on us. The love He has for us is greater than the love we have for each other."

"Speaking of love; I don't want you to go through with this plan of yours. Handing yourself over ain't the way to go. Kazimir's not gonna kill you quickly. He'll torture you and keep you alive for as long as he can. That's the type of person he is.

"He probably didn't give a damn about Laska. It's the principle of it. You killed one of his kin. So, he'll make an example outta you. To send a message, to discourage anyone else from trying him. You really wanna face that?"

"I don't have a choice. She's everything to me. It's my fault he's dead. She tried to get me to leave but I didn't listen. I thought about all the nasty things he did to her. The things he would continue to do. He had to go. Just promise me you'll keep her safe. When she wakes up and finds that I'm gone. You won't let her come after me. Promise me, brother."

"You don't need me to say it. You already know I'll keep her safe."

"Thank you."

Jedrek walks over to Raisa and kisses her on the forehead. She smiles at him and drifts back into slumber.

"Goodbye, my lyubov," Jedrek whispers.

Rafiq waits by the door.

"This doesn't feel right. I should be going out in a blaze of glory with you."

Jedrek puts his hand on Rafiq's shoulder.

"You're her brother too and she'll need you more than I do. This is the last favor I'll ever ask you. Don't let her outta your sight; no matter what it takes."

Rafiq nods his head.

"I promise."

They hug.

"You're gonna walk all the way to town?"

"The easiest way to get caught. Besides, you'll need the car to get to where you're going."

"Maybe I should dig Rell up and see if his keys are in his pocket."

"No thanks, I'd rather walk."

"There's so much I wanna say but I can't find the words."

"You don't have to say anything. It's better this way."

Jedrek opens the door.

"We all die in the end. At least I get to choose the time and place I meet my end."

Chapter 42

Rafiq watches Jedrek walk down the street until he's out of sight.

"May God be with you my brother," Rafiq says closing the door.

Jedrek walks for miles entirely unnoticed. Maybe he should've hidden in plain sight. He laughs at the thought. Jedrek arrives at the bus stop.

Since he's made it this far without being seen. Perhaps he can go a little farther, he considers. Jedrek waits patiently for the bus. A lady walks up, but she hesitates to sit down on the bench next to Jedrek.

"I can stand if you'd like to sit," Jedrek suggests.

She clutches her purse. Jedrek shakes his head. The bus stops, and the woman hurries to board as if being chased by Jedrek. It's not until Jedrek steps on the bus that he remembers he doesn't have any money.

The bus driver looks at Jedrek's bandaged hand and dirty clothes.

"What happened to you? Were you attacked?" The bus driver politely asks.

"Yes," Jedrek answers.

"I'm sorry to hear that. Do you need medical attention?"

"No."

"Well take a seat."

"I can't. I don't have any money to pay the fare."

"This ride's on me. Take a seat."

"Thank you."

"You're welcome."

Jedrek sits at the back of the bus alone. He reflects on the events that have taken place.

"Is this really happening? Or is this some bad dream that I can't wake up from? Yesterday my biggest concern was possibly having to fire an employee. Today I'm being hunted by the Russian Mafia. They say God works in mysterious ways. I'm hoping that whatever happens, is meant to happen for the benefit of my wife.

"Maybe God is gonna use me; my sacrifice to make sure she's safe. I hope that by giving myself up she can finally be free of all this madness. I'm sorry Raisa. I'm truly sorry for leaving you like this. You've been through a lot. I never intended to add widow to your list of woes. But I have to do this. I have to distract them long enough for you to escape. I have to put my life on the line.

"Because they're not gonna stop chasing us. But I'm hoping they'll leave you alone once they have me. I hope that one day you'll find peace and happiness. Out of all the things in this world that I love about you. Your smile is what I cherish the most. While they're torturing me, I'll have the memory of your smile to provide comfort through the pain.

"Comfort in knowing that you'll live, and one day be able to smile that beautiful smile again. I believe Rafiq will get you away from here. He promised me. He wouldn't go back on his word, he never has. You'll try to follow me, but Ra will stop you. I hope you won't be too upset with him. I hope you won't be upset with me for not giving you a choice in the matter."

Jedrek glances at the family sitting in the middle. The man hugs his woman with one arm and holds the little girl sitting on his lap with the other. Jedrek smiles.

"That should've been us. That could've been us. That would've been us. It wouldn't have mattered if it were a boy or a girl. As long as the baby was healthy. I could hear us right now having a playful disagreement over baby names. I wouldn't suggest Jedrek Junior. if it were a boy. I think one person with a terrible name like Jedrek is enough. I'd rub your belly and talk to our unborn child.

"I'd massage your feet and cook your meals. I'd go to all your doctor's appointments with you. I could picture us shopping for baby clothes and supplies. I'd be in the delivery room holding your hand during childbirth. I'd be honored to cut the umbilical cord. I'm picturing our beautiful light-skinned curly-haired baby. Maybe we would've discussed having another baby someday.

"Foolish dreams I suppose. I shouldn't sit here and think about what could've been when I know it'll never be. I don't regret my decision, but it would've been a beautiful life. You have a chance to live.

You're still young and you have your whole life ahead of you. I want you to go on living for both of us. Kazimir will believe he's won but I win. Going to face my death is not how I win. Your survival is my victory."

The bus cruises by Jedrek's shop. Jedrek does a doubletake at the devastation of his shop.

"Now I see why Ra didn't care about the ownership transfer. He knew how much the shop meant to me. That's why he didn't tell me. I find it ironic that Ra does bad things and yet he's never been comfortable giving bad news. Unfortunately for you, Raisa will be awake soon and you'll have to give her the bad news.

"She's the nicest woman and it usually takes a lot to upset her. This will hit hard. I don't know how she'll react. I hope you can see her through this difficult time. I wanna go back to the place where it all started. Where we first met. If I could just make it there. If I could just see it, one last time. It'll be a pale substitute for not being able to share these final moments with you. But it's all I have left."

The bus comes to a stop. Jedrek decides to get off there.

"Say, young man, whatever you're going through. God won't put more on you than you can bear. Just continue to seek Him. Whatever you need God's got it," the driver says.

"Amen sir," Jedrek says.

"Here."

The bus driver hands Jedrek some money.

"It's not much. Maybe you can get yourself a cup of coffee and a sandwich or something."

"Thank you, sir."

"May God Bless you."

"May God Bless you, sir."

Jedrek is close to his destination, no more than a block away.

"He's right. I've been too busy thinking about my wife. I haven't stopped to pray. Heavenly Father I wanna thank you for Blessing me. Thank you for Blessing me with the strength to do this. Thank you for keeping me safe. I pray that you'll continue to Bless my family, my beautiful wife Raisa, my brother Rafiq, and Burn. I pray that you'll continue to keep them safe.

"I pray that you'll comfort my wife. I pray she finds solace in the days to come. I'm grateful to have been blessed with such a wonderful woman, if only for a short time. I'd be lying if I said I was sorry for killing that weasel. And yet I pray you'll forgive me for it because it was a sin. I pray that if I must be punished, I'll suffer at Kazimir's hands now and not suffer in hell for eternity. I pray in Jesus' name, Amen."

Jedrek looks up at the sign in front of the restaurant.

"Rada's Bistro, I made it. Thank you, Jesus. This is where we met. Where you changed my life."

Jedrek enters the restaurant.

"Oh my God! Rada, come quick!" The hostess exclaims at the sight of Jedrek.

"What is it?" Rada asks coming from the kitchen.

Rada jumps when she sees Jedrek.

"Jedrek? Are you ok?" Rada asks.

"I'm fine."

"What happened to you? Where is Raisa? Is she ok?"

"She's fine."

"I was worried sick about her when she did not show up to work or call in. I knew something was wrong because that is unlike her. Were you in an accident?"

"May I have a table please?"

"Sure, will Raisa be joining you?"

"No, just me."

"I will show you to your table. Follow me," Rada says grabbing a menu.

Jedrek spots an employee of the month picture of Raisa on the wall. He smiles.

"There's that smile."

"This way Jedrek," Rada says.

Rada seats Jedrek in a booth next to the far wall.

"Are you ready to order?" She asks.

"I don't have that much money, so I'll just have a cup of coffee."

"You can order anything you like. It's on the house.

She hands him a menu.

"I don't have much of an appetite."

"I'll make you something special," she says taking the menu back.

Jedrek begins to fantasize about Raisa.

"You'd probably be sitting here making faces at me or trying to tickle me. There was never a dull moment with you around. You're all I ever wanted in this world. You're everything a man could ever hope for in a wife."

Rada returns with a hot cup of coffee.

"Two sugars with a little cream; just how you like it," Rada says.

A waitress ushers in two guys wearing expensive suits. She points to Rada.

"I'm sorry Jedrek but you shouldn't have come here. Here he is," she tells the men.

Jedrek smiles at her.

"I knew something was up with you when you kept asking about Raisa. And to think she cares about you."

"And I, her."

"Yeah right."

"This is nothing personal, this is business."

"I pray God has mercy on you."

Rada steps back. The men close in brandishing their weapons.

"Don't move," one of them says.

The other patrons begin to panic.

"Don't be alarmed, we're police officers," the man adds.

Jedrek closes his eyes.

"Raisa my love, I don't want you to miss me."

The man hits Jedrek in the face with the gun knocking him unconscious.

Chapter 43

"Jeed...Jeed!" Raisa awakes.

"Oh crap," Rafiq utters.

Raisa looks around the room.

"Jeed!"

"It's all right. You were probably having a nightmare," Rafiq says.

"Where's Jeed?"

Rafiq looks down at his shoes. He can't bring himself to look Raisa in the eye.

"Where is my husband?"

"He's gone."

"Gone where?"

"He went to give himself up."

"What?! No...no. You're joking and it isn't funny."

"It's no joke."

"Why would he do that? Why didn't you stop him?"

"I tried to talk him out of it?"

"Talk? You didn't try hard enough. You're supposed to be his brother."

"I am."

"How can you call yourself that? He's alone out there. I must go."

Rafiq blocks her path.

"I can't let you do that."

"Get out of my way or I'll kick you in the nuts."

"Jed told me to stop you from going after him."

"You'll stop me, but you couldn't stop him. How are you going to live with yourself if something happens to him? We must stop him, it's not too late."

"He's been gone for a while. He might even…"

"Don't say it! He's not!"

"I'm sorry. Try to understand he did it for you. He did it to protect you."

"I understand, but do you? Have you ever loved someone more than anything? To you he's Jed. To me, he's the sun and without his light, there's nothing but darkness. So please…let me go."

Rafiq shakes his head.

"No, I can't. He made me promise."

Raisa drops her head and sobs.

"Ra," Burn says with compassion in his voice.

Burn points at Raisa encouraging Rafiq to show sympathy.

"I know this is hard on you. I can't imagine how you must feel but I do care. And I'm here for you."

Rafiq puts his hand on Raisa's shoulder. She grabs him and pulls him in close for a tight squeeze hug. Unbeknownst to Rafiq, Raisa reaches for his gun. She snatches away and points the gun at him. Rafiq looks at Burn with a suckered expression.

"Put the gun down miss," Burn pleads.

Raisa points the gun at Burn.

"Be quiet Burn," she responds.

"Hey, look I'm on your side. I didn't have anything to do with your man leaving. I was asleep when he left. So please point that gun somewhere else."

"Really Burn, you're gonna play me like that?" Rafiq questions.

"Hey, I'm just saying I can see from both of y'all perspectives," Burn says.

"I can see you shut the hell up," Rafiq says.

"Whatever man," Burn retorts.

"Please put the gun down before you hurt yourself," Rafiq cautions.

"Give me your keys," Raisa says turning the gun on Rafiq.

"My keys? Ok."

Rafiq reaches into his pocket and throws the keys on the floor at Raisa's feet. She kneels to pick them up.

"I know you didn't just give her my keys?" Burns asks.

"Don't worry about it. She's not going anywhere," Rafiq says.

"Why?" Raisa asks.

"Because you don't know where Kazimir is and I'm not telling you," Rafiq explains.

"Tell me where he is!" Raisa exclaims.

"No, and if you shoot me, you still won't get the information."

Burn smiles.

"So put the gun down and let's talk this over," Rafiq suggests.

"Give me your phone," Raisa orders.

"What do you want with my phone?" Rafiq asks.

"You were in contact with Kazimir earlier. Give me your phone," she reiterates.

"This phone?"

Rafiq waves the phone at her.

"You'll have to pry it from my cold dead hands. 'Cause I'm not giving it to you. I promised my brother I'd keep you safe and I'm keeping that promise."

Raisa closes her eyes and squeezes the trigger, shooting Rafiq in the chest. Rafiq goes down and the phone slides to Raisa. She picks it up.

"Damn! I can't believe you shot me!" Rafiq yells.

"Are you all, right?" Raisa asks.

Rafiq, thankful he was still wearing his bulletproof vest looks up at her. Burn looks on in shock.

"Oh snap! That chick just shot at you with her eyes closed," Burn says.

"Did you shoot at me with your eyes closed?"

"I was afraid. I don't like guns, but you left me no choice. Don't try to stop me," she says still pointing the gun at Rafiq.

"Don't do it. I'm not even mad that you shot me. Just don't go," Rafiq says.

"I'm leaving now. Move," she says.

"I see there's no way I can convince you to stay. So, let me go with you. I'll help you bring him back. I swear," Rafiq says.

"You lie. Move! She warns.

Rafiq crawls across the floor.

"Don't do this," Burn begs.

"I have to; he's my love, my life, my everything."

Raisa exits the house and climbs into the car. Burn and Rafiq watch anxiously from the door. Perhaps too worried she'll accidentally shoot one of them in the head should they try to stop her again. She starts the car and drives away.

"I just got punked by a petite Russian lady, with my own gun. Let's not mention this to anyone," Rafiq says.

"I can't believe you gave her my keys."

"Shut up, it's your fault Hype and Rell found us in the first place."

"How you figure that?"

"I didn't tell those fools about this safe house. They must've found out from you. You used to get high with those clowns."

Burn smiles.

"My fault, I might've let it slip out."

"Yeah, I hope she wrecks your damn car too."

"That's messed up."

"Let me see your phone. I'm gonna call a cab."

"My phone was in the car."

"Are you serious?"

"Does it look like I'm joking?"

Rafiq stomps.

"Damn! We gotta go after her," Rafiq insists.

"Yeah, but how?"

Rafiq looks at the shovel.

"I guess I'll have to dig up ole Rell and see if he's holding those keys."

Burn shakes his head.

Chapter 44

Raisa turns her phone on for the first time since yesterday. She primarily uses her phone to communicate with Jedrek when they're apart from one another. Her phone buzzes with notifications of messages from Rada and others at the bistro. She ignores the messages and immediately tries to call Jedrek. It goes straight to voicemail.

She can't recall if Jedrek had his phone or left it at the house when they fled. It all happened so fast. Time is of the essence and Jedrek's life hangs in the balance. She's nervous to call Kazimir but she knows it's necessary. She can't afford to waste any more time with Jedrek having a head start. She decides to use her phone to call Kazimir, knowing he won't recognize the number.

Calling directly from Rafiq's phone would admit his involvement. She makes it a point not to involve Rafiq and Burn. Although she's upset with them, she doesn't wish them any harm. Raisa searches through Rafiq's disposable cell phone; casually swerving in the other lane. She searches for Kazimir's name in the list of "contacts." She quickly realizes there are no names listed in "contacts."

She tries the "call logs" and finds nearly a dozen different numbers. She notices Jedrek's phone number amid the others. She strokes the screen.

"I'm coming my love," she says.

Using her phone, she dials the most recently used number in Rafiq's phone. 'You are roaming, to call your mobile carrier or any other phone number, purchase a calling pin by pressing 1 now. To make a collect call to a mobile phone or a landline phone dial 2 now,' the message prompts. She drops the phone in the seat.

"Jedrek, you don't know what you've done to me. I was alone. I didn't have the love of my family. I was in a very dark place. Then you came into my life. You showed me, love, I never thought existed. You allowed me to feel safe for the first time since I left Russia. I fear there is no safe place without you. I don't want to go back to the darkness. You're my husband, my best friend, my hero.

"You didn't just save me from Laska. You saved my life every day. Some people go their whole lives searching for the right person. I was Blessed to find my true love early on. I'd hoped we would grow old together. I would've loved nothing more than to bear your children. Raise a family and live long enough to see our children raise their own families. I would miss you so much if I lost you.

"I should be upset with you, but I can't imagine how you felt when you left me. You probably felt the loneliness I feel. It's real; it aches. My heart aches for you Jeed. If something happens to you it would be my fault. I would've ruined your life. If your grandmother were here, she would hate me for getting you into this mess. If I never agreed to meet Laska that night.

"If I'd never been so stupid to ignore my father's warning. You would be somewhere safe. If only I could go back in time. You and I would have never met. I would never have known your heart, but you'd be safe. Father God, I pray you'll Bless my husband. I pray you'll protect him from harm."

Raisa grabs the phone and redials.

"What up?" A man asks.

"I want to speak to Kazimir," Raisa says.

"There's no Kazimir here but you sound cute though," the man responds.

"Ugh!"

Raisa hangs up. She recalls the phone conversation Rafiq had with Kazimir earlier that morning. She surveys for the phone number coinciding with that time frame. She spies the number she believes to be Kazimir's. Once again, she uses her phone to dial, pausing to glance at the road.

"Hello," a man answers with a thick Russian accent.

"Zdravstvuyte Kazimir, Raisa says.

"Who is this?"

"Raisa Mann."

Kazimir laughs.

"The little girl who ran away from home. Where have you been hiding little girl? To what do I owe the pleasure?"

"I want to make a deal."

"You call to surrender, yes?" Tell me, how did you come by this phone number?"

"It doesn't matter. The only thing that matters is my husband."

"Your husband will be dead soon."

"You have him?"

"Of course."

"Take me instead."

"What would I want with a mud duck whore like you?"

"We can do without the insults."

Kazimir laughs.

"You have spirit, I like that," he says.

"I don't care what happens to me but don't hurt my husband."

"You would trade your life for that animal? You disgust me."

"This coming from someone who forces women into doing unspeakable acts."

"Watch what you say to me girl, or your husband will be dead before I hang up."

"No don't! Please, I'll do anything you want if you let him go."

"Deal."

"You promise you'll let him go?"

"I'll release him once I have you in my possession; I promise."

"Where can I find you?"

"Nice try but I'm not giving you, my location. I'll arrange a proper escort for you."

"I don't trust your nasty men."

"You have my word. They will not harm you unless you give them cause to."

"Ok, where do you want me to meet them?"

"Go to Rada's Bistro."

"Why Rada's Bistro?"

"Easy for you to find. After all, there is where we found your husband. Be sure to come alone. Any funny business and you'll never see your husband again; understood?"

"Yes."

"Good, I'll see you shortly."

Kazimir hangs up. Raisa places the phone in the seat.

"He went back to the place where we met. I love that wonderful man. It angers me to hear Kazimir say such horrible things. He's jealous of our love. He's jealous of you because you're beautiful and strong. I doubt Kazimir can do 100 pushups with me on his back as

234

you can. Oh, how I'll miss exercising with you. I'll miss the piggyback rides through the park. You, always calling me out for sniffing your neck and me denying ever doing it.

"You know I love the smell of your cologne. You'd spray it on heavy just for me. I remember our first date. I was so nervous because I wanted everything to go well. You seemed so calm and relaxed. You were very charming. You made me feel comfortable and I let my guard down. It was a special night. A night we didn't want to end.

"We stayed up until sunrise talking about the future and what we wanted out of life. I would've thought that after so much time together. You would've tried to kiss me goodbye, but not you. You were a gentleman to the very end. I so wanted to kiss you. By not kissing me, you made me want you even more. I went to work the following day and told Rada I was in love. She laughed at me.

"She told me you only wanted one thing. I love that you respected my decision to wait until marriage. You were so patient with me. You never laughed at my old-fashioned beliefs. You never once tried to pressure me or complain. You simply went with the flow. You proposed to me in front of everyone at the bistro. You made me the happiest woman in the world that day.

"You also taught Rada a valuable lesson, not to judge a book by its cover. Our wedding day was blissful. The moment you said your vows. I knew I would love you forever. I knew I would devote my life to you, even die for you. I always knew you were willing to sacrifice yourself for me. But I won't have that, at any cost. You'll be upset with my decision. I hope you won't try to resist.

"I hope you won't try to find me and rescue me once I'm gone. If you go peacefully, they will let you live. Don't be the hero that I know you are. This time I need you to run and don't look back."

Raisa sheds a tear.

"I regret keeping my shame a secret. I hope you know I never kept any other secrets from you. The only secret I held, and you already knew about it."

She laughs.

"It's unbelievable how well you know me. It just proves once again that we were meant to be. I've laid awake on occasion and watched you sleep. I thought to myself, it's hard to believe you're real. The man of my dreams made true. You sometimes smile in your sleep. I wonder what you dream about. I'd like to think you were dreaming about us; maybe having children.

"Maybe you dream about your mom and grandma. You know for a strong man; you have such a cute little snore."

She giggles.

"The small intimate details are what I shall miss the most. Like when you gave me the sad puppy dog face. To try to persuade me to get out of the house. It's not that I didn't like going out. I cherish every moment I spent with you. But you never had to do any of that stuff to please me. I could think of much better ways to spend the time.

"I'd much rather cuddle with you on the couch than sit in a crowded movie theater. I never liked the idea of sharing you with all those other people. When we were at home I had you all to myself. Sitting there with my head on your lap listening to you read scripture with your deep voice; always made me melt. Our wrestling matches were the most fun.

"I'd use any excuse I could to feel your body pressed against mine. Even go as far as annoying you, just to get you riled up. I'm still undefeated by the way."

Her smile turns into a frown.

"You can still have those things with someone else if you choose. As much as it pains me to think about you with another woman, I honestly hope you find someone that makes you happy. It would please me to know there's somebody there to take care of you. To know there's somebody there to erase the pain I've caused. I'm truly sorry my love."

Raisa slams on the brakes. She's in disbelief at the sight of the shop.

"Those savages!"

She pounds her fist on the dashboard.

"Jeed worked so hard to establish this business. For some heartless brutes to destroy in moments what took time to build; is just cruel. I know someone saw who did this but no one will help. That's how it goes.

237

You gave everyone that came to the shop a break. And this is how the neighborhood thanks you."

She lets out a sigh of despair.

"Jeed you will have to move on. Maybe you can find another place to set up shop. You're too good for this town anyway. You're a smart and resourceful man. You can build an even better shop."

The driver behind Raisa honks the horn at her. She rolls the window down and politely waves the motorist on. The driver continues to honk the horn.

"Get the hell out the road dumbass," a man shouts from the car.

Raisa holds the gun out the window. The man throws his car in reverse and speeds off in the opposite direction.

"Wrong girl, wrong day buddy."

She checks the rearview mirror.

"I wonder if Rafiq saw this and yet he was still willing to give us the money? If that's the case, it would be difficult to be upset with him. I almost feel bad for shooting him. Jeed made it to Rada's. Then he might have seen it too."

She shakes her head.

"My man's been through so much. For the devil to trouble you so; God must have a special purpose for you. I'll make sure you live to fulfill it."

She drives on, taking in one last look at the shop's remains.

"I should have come to work with you. There wasn't a day that went by I didn't ponder it. I would've loved to work alongside you. You know I could never get enough of being around you. I wanted to give you space. Absence makes the heart grow fonder. You know that old saying. I figured I'd get in the way.

"I didn't want to cause any issues between you and your employees. Now I regret not quitting my job. If I'd known our time together would be cut short. I would've spent every moment with you. I'm afraid of what's to come. To have you and then to not have you; is a fate worse than death. I don't know how I'll endure it. I pray for strength in Jesus' name, Amen. I hope they'll let me see you one last time.

"I would tell you I hold up my ring finger to show you, I'll always honor being your wife. I would tell you how much I love you as opposed to saying goodbye. I would smile at you. So that your last memory of me would be a good one."

Raisa parks the car around the corner from the bistro. She doesn't want to risk being seen in Burn's car.

"He said no funny business. So, I guess I won't be needing this."

She places the gun under the driver's seat.

"Rafiq had good intentions. He was only trying to help his brother. It must've been hard for him to watch Jeed go off by his lonesome. He was asked to stop worrying about a man he knew most of his life. To protect a woman, he barely knows. That's admirable."

Raisa puts the car keys in the sun visor.

"Just like in the American films," she says.

She proceeds to the bistro.

"Speaking of movies, I rather enjoyed watching horror movies with you. Eighties classic horrors became my favorite. We would laugh at the fake gory scenes and all the pointless nudity. You told me it was ok to laugh when the black guy dies first because he got paid for it. You have a logical way of thinking."

Raisa stops at the door. She hesitates

"I guess this is the end of the road for me. Probably the last time I'll ever see this place."

She closes her eyes and exhales slowly.

"I can do this. I must."

She enters and sees two men hanging around the hostess stand. Adira spots Raisa. She frantically shakes her head to warn Raisa. The men turn around.

"Don't move," the taller man orders.

The man opens his jacket revealing his Desert Eagle .44 Magnum.

"Big tough guy like you, afraid of a girl weighing 52 kilograms? Raisa teases.

The man smirks and closes his jacket.

"Let's get this show on the road," the other man says motioning to the door.

"I'm sorry Raisa," Adira says.

"It's ok," Raisa reassures her.

"Wait!" Rada says.

"What now?" The taller man asks.

"How much do I get for this one?" Rada asks.

"There is no bounty for the girl," the other man says.

"You have been rewarded. Don't be greedy," the taller man says.

"Rada, you gave up my husband?"

Rada is speechless.

"Say it isn't so," Raisa demands.

"You brought it on yourselves," Rada answers.

"You jezebel!"

Raisa lunges at Rada. The taller man grabs her and pulls her back.

"Don't let her get me," Rada pleads.

"Take your filthy hands off me," Raisa demands.

"We were told not to be rough with you if you were good. Are you good?" The taller man asks.

"Yes, I'm good. Let me go," Raisa responds.

The man releases his grip. Raisa decks Rada with a strong right hook, knocking her to the floor.

"Now I'm good. Now we can go."

The men laugh.

"Rada you should learn to duck," the taller man says.

"Maybe she should use some of the money on karate lessons," the other man suggests.

Rada is too woozy to get up or maybe too afraid. She looks up at Raisa.

"That was for my husband," Raisa says with teary eyes.

"Come now," the taller man tells Raisa.

"Jeed, they can take my body, but my heart will always be yours."

Chapter 45

Jedrek was taken to a warehouse overlooking the docks. Somewhat of a shipping magnate, Kazimir runs the docks. One of his many business fronts. Jedrek is brought into an office on the third floor. A hulking man with salt and pepper hair, sporting an eyepatch stands next to the door. A tall slender man with gray hair leans against the wall.

"You must be Jedrek Mann," the man sitting in the swivel chair says spinning around.

Jedrek looks at the tall slender man.

"Yes," Jedrek answers.

"Why are you looking at him?" The man asks.

"Because he's the boss," Jedrek explains.

The man laughs.

"And what brought you to that conclusion?" The man continues.

"When I walked in you had your back to the door. No one so notorious would sit with their back to the door."

The tall slender man makes eye contact with Jedrek.

"You're very clever. I am Kazimir," says the tall slender man.

"Why the ruse?" Jedrek asks.

"I didn't feel you were worth my attention, but I was wrong. You seem clever enough to have killed my nephew Laska. Is that so?"

Jedrek nods his head yes.

"Let me hear you say you killed Laska," Kazimir commands.

"I killed him."

"And do you regret it?"

"I regret the outcome."

"You have balls. I'll give you that."

"There's no need for me to beg. You're gonna kill me anyway."

"Before it's all over, you'll beg."

"Do you believe killing me will bring you triumph?"

"Do you believe giving your life will settle the score? His name was Laska, say it."

Jedrek stands firm. Kazimir smiles.

"Valor, eh? A word of advice, don't mistake foolishness for bravery. I'm going to educate you before you die. Now pay attention. This is a story of legends.

Jedrek yields his attention to Kazimir.

"Years ago, in Moscow, I ran with a tight little crew. There were four of us petty crooks; trying to make a name for ourselves. We obeyed no laws and we lived by only one code. That code was brotherhood; never forsaking one another. We had a few successful minor heists, but we were looking for a big score. We managed to catch the attention of a key player. Big Serg is what they called him.

"Not because of his stature but because he had enough firepower to level a mountain. Big Serg was feared throughout Moscow. My crew and I idolized him. We wanted to be like him. So, we jumped at the opportunity to work for him. 'This is no kiddie stuff,' he warned us. We told him we were ready. There was no turning back. He told us of a deal going down involving one of his competitors.

"Our job was to go in and take the money. If we were successful, we would become a part of his organization. If we were caught, Big Serg didn't know us, and we didn't know him. It was simple. We went in and made it out with the money. There were more men waiting for us outside. Nikita was our lookout that night and they had the drop on him. It was against the code to leave one of ours behind.

"So, we gave ourselves up. They knew someone put us up to it. Only the heavy hitters knew what went on there. They tried to get us to talk. Half a day went by; they tortured us mercilessly."

Kazimir points at the man wearing an eyepatch.

"Poor Odin over there lost his eye during the ordeal. We knew we were dead either way. They could not break us with pain. They resorted to dirty tactics. One of the men knew of Nikita's family from a picture he carried in his pocket. A picture of his girlfriend Mariska and their daughter Rada. The man said they would visit Mariska's house.

"They would take turns raping the girls and when they were done, they would kill them. The threat broke Nikita. He gave up Big Serg's name. The men cut Nikita loose and took him away. Then we heard Nikita scream worse than before. Moments later Big Serg walked into the room holding Nikita's head. 'Congratulations, you have passed the test,' he said.

"The robbery and the torture were all orchestrated by Big Serg to initiate us into his organization. He claimed he killed Nikita because he was weak and stupid. That was the first time I heard that saying, don't mistake foolishness for bravery. I heard his message loud and clear. Would you like to know what happened to Big Serg?"

"No, but I get the feeling you're gonna tell me anyway," Jedrek says.

"Big Serg lived and died like a king. I cut his head off myself. After all, he killed Nikita and we were like brothers."

"That story has nothing to do with me," Jedrek says.

"It's no coincidence you were discovered at Rada's Bistro. You give yourself up in hopes that I will spare your wife. You would face certain doom for a woman, just like Nikita."

"For love, the greatest cause of all," Jedrek responds.

"You'll regret ever meeting that woman."

"I could never."

"You will after we're done with you."

"Cut the crap. If you want me here I am. Just you and me or are you too afraid to fight me like a man?"

The man standing next to Jedrek draws his fist back. Kazimir throws his hand up.

"Leave it. Don't you see what he's doing? He's trying to bait us into finishing him quickly. Isn't that right monkey?" Kazimir asks.

The men laugh at Jedrek. Jedrek scowls at Kazimir.

"You see I can talk trash too. Let me know when it sinks in. That moment you realize how screwed you are."

"You can take my life, but you can't take my soul."

"That's it? No last-ditch heroics? How disappointing."

A man walks in and whispers something to Kazimir. They look at Jedrek.

"Bring her in," Kazimir orders the man.

The man leaves.

"Now the fun begins," Kazimir says.

"Let's get this over with," Jedrek says.

"You're not afraid to die, are you?"

"If it's God's Will, then so it shall be done. I have faith in God that I'll be with Him in paradise when it's over."

"There are worst things than death. You'll know what that means in just a moment."

Kazimir points at the door as it slowly opens. Jedrek is stunned to see Raisa standing in the doorway. Jedrek looks at Kazimir. Kazimir smiles.

"Step forward," Odin tells Raisa.

She rushes to Jedrek's arms.

"Did they hurt you?" Jedrek asks.

"No, I'm fine," she responds.

She pushes him.

"Why did you leave me?" She asks.

She pulls him closer for a tighter hug.

"I'm sorry," he says holding her tight.

"How touching," Kazimir says.

"Let my wife go. She didn't kill your nephew, I did."

"She's just as guilty as you are," Kazimir explains.

"You said you'd release my husband if I gave myself up."

"Why would you do that?" Jedrek asks.

"For the same reason you did; because of love," she says touching his face.

"I'm a man of my word. I will release your husband," Kazimir says.

"I'm not going anywhere without my wife."

"You mistake my intentions. I'm releasing you from this world."

"You tricked me!" Raisa exclaims.

"Whatever you're gonna do to me, my wife doesn't need to see it. I don't want her to see that!" Jedrek says looking around the room at the other men.

"She gets a front-row seat. Then after that, I'll put her to work."

"My wife is no slave to anyone."

"She belongs to me now. Is it beginning to sink in?" Kazimir asks.

"I only wanted to protect my wife. You would've done the same thing."

"If you're trying to appeal to my humanity. I'm far removed from remorse or redemption."

Raisa notices a picture of Galina on Kazimir's desk.

"The photograph, that's Galina. What have you done with her?" Raisa asks.

"Galina is my daughter."

Raisa is astonished.

"Don't look so surprised. You had to have known she was a part of my organization."

"But she helped me escape," Raisa says.

"Did she? Or did she tell you to go to Rada's Bistro, where she would come to claim you for her own? You see my Galina has always favored cake over sausage. She went against the grain and decided to keep you as a pet."

"But she was so nice to me."

"Then she was doing her job. Laska was tasked with showing her the ropes, so she could take over supervising the girls. I found his mistreatment of the girls to be appalling."

"Then release them," Raisa says.

"Human trafficking exists with or without Kazimir. Yet, someone must be in control. Why not Kazimir?"

"You're not in control. In the end, you're just a slave to the devil," Jedrek says.

"Jedrek Mann, I am the devil, and your wife is a slave to me. Consigned by her own free will."

Jedrek looks at Raisa.

"You're not making my wife a slave."

"There's nothing you can do to stop it."

"I'll kill any man that tries it," Jedrek warns.

"Please, this is no comic book, and you are no superhero. I'll show you. Obman! Take the girl, right here, right now.

Obman stands up from Kazimir's desk.

"Don't try it," Jedrek says.

With a smirk, Obman reaches for Raisa. Jedrek punches Obman knocking one of his teeth out. He collapses to the floor. Odin points his gun at Jedrek.

"No, aim the gun at the girl," Kazimir suggests.

Jedrek extends his arm in front of Raisa.

"You'll have to kill me," he says.

"No! This ends now! Raisa exclaims gripping Jedrek's arm.

Kazimir signals Odin to lower his weapon.

"Your nephew was not an honorable man, and neither are you for seeking to avenge him."

"What do you know of honor girl? I granted your freedom when you escaped."

"Free will is not yours to give," Raisa says.

"I've always known where you were. I could have come for you at any time. I allowed you to keep your freedom. An act born from Galina's plea. She felt that if she couldn't have you, nobody deserved to. I honored her request then I sent her away."

"You sent her away?" Raisa asks.

"Yes, I sent her away out of disappointment. She fell in love with a slave. A foolish mistake like that could get you killed. Her little stunt got Laska busted. After which, I bailed him out and made him lay low. Not too soon after Laska made his way back to town, you killed him."

"He left me no choice, he threatened my wife," Jedrek explains.

"Because she provoked him."

"I did no such thing," Raisa says.

"That's not what I heard," Kazimir says.

"Who told you that? Jedrek asks.

Kazimir looks at Raisa.

"Klavdii told me everything," Kazimir says.

"You mean that big creep with your nephew? I'm sure he didn't tell you the truth. Like the fact, your nephew came after me for revenge."

"He was told to stay away from you," Kazimir explains.

"She's lying to save her ass," Odin says.

"What need would I have to lie now? You'll probably kill us anyway."

"Perhaps," Kazimir says.

"I heard your nephew and that man plotting to kill you and take over."

"I want to hear what Klavdii has to say to that accusation. Odin, bring in Klavdii. We'll get down to the bottom of this. In the meantime, boys pick Obman up."

Two men help Obman up and sit him in a chair. Obman glances at Jedrek, dazed and angry. Jedrek wraps his arms around Raisa. Kazimir smiles at her. She rolls her eyes at him. Klavdii staggers in with Odin jamming a gun in his back. Odin forces Klavdii into a chair. Kazimir sits on the edge of his desk.

"Klavdii, I have a problem," Kazimir says.

"If it's those two I'll be happy to kill them for you," Klavdii hints at Jedrek and Raisa.

Kazimir nods his head at Odin. Odin thumps Klavdii in the back of the head with the butt of the gun.

"You speak when spoken to," Odin says.

"Sorry boss," Klavdii says.

Odin strikes him again. Kazimir scoffs.

"You never learn," Kazimir says.

Klavdii nods his head.

"Good, you can teach a dumb dog new tricks. Well, you remember Raisa. But I don't think you've had the pleasure of meeting her husband Jedrek. He admits to killing Laska. That alone is enough to kill him. The problem is they are claiming Laska forced Jedrek's hand. And that doesn't coincide with the story you told me earlier."

Odin strikes Klavdii again.

"Now would be your time to speak!" Kazimir shouts.

"They're lying, she set Laska up somehow," Klavdii responds.

Kazimir looks at Raisa prompting a response.

Your nephew came into Rada's Bistro a couple of days ago. The following day I saw him at the church. Then he came to our home to kidnap me," Raisa explains.

Kazimir looks at Klavdii.

"Laska was advised to stay away from Rada's Bistro. Did he ignore my order? Kazimir asks.

"We didn't go to Rada's. Laska didn't even like the food there," Klavdii responds.

"Did Laska go to church?" Kazimir asks.

"Laska would not be caught dead in a church. Pardon my expression boss," Klavdii says.

"Did Laska go to their home?" Kazimir asks.

"Yes, but as I said before he only meant to scare her," Klavdii answers.

"You, lying bastard," Raisa says.

"Settle down girl," Kazimir warns her.

"We're getting nowhere. You should just let me kill all three of them," Odin suggests.

"This is why you're not in charge my old comrade. Besides, I want to know the truth," Kazimir says.

Kazimir looks at Raisa.

"Girl, why did you stay after you escaped capture? You could have gone home to your family," Kazimir says.

"I thought about it every day. But I couldn't risk putting them in danger. The less they knew the better," Raisa explains.

Kazimir nods his head in understanding. Then he turns his attention to Klavdii.

"Raisa tells me she overheard you and Laska plotting to kill me; take control of my territories. What do you have to say to that?"

"It's a lie, boss! I swear on my father's grave, it's a lie!" Klavdii declares.

"I promise you it's the truth," Raisa responds.

"Boss, I've served you for years. You selected me to guard your nephew," Klavdii reminds him.

"And look how well that worked out," Kazimir says.

"Boss you know me."

"I know you're replaceable."

"You're going to take the word of a slave over me?"

"Watch what you say about the missus in front of her husband. He's willing to kill for her."

Kazimir turns to Raisa.

"I almost believe you. A part of me wants to believe you," Kazimir tells her.

"What more can I say? I've told you everything," Raisa says.

"Give me more details about the alleged conversation, between Laska and Klavdii. What was said word for word," Kazimir urges.

"Ok, there was me and another girl in the back seat," Raisa says.

"And what became of this other girl? Are you hiding her someplace?" Kazimir asks.

"No, and she had nothing to do with what happened. So, leave her out of this."

"Very well, but you're running out of time. Continue."

"Klavdii was nervous. 'I can't shake this feeling,' he told Laska. 'Grab hold of your balls and be a man,' Laska replied. 'What if the boss finds out about what we've done?' Klavdii asked. 'He won't find out,' Laska assured him. 'But if he does, he will punish us for disobeying him,' Klavdii cautioned. 'Not if he's dead,' Laska said. 'What?' Klavdii asked. 'I've been thinking, maybe it's time for new leadership.

"Kazimir is old, and he's gone soft,' Laska said. 'You're seriously going to make a move against Kazimir? It would be suicide; he has the numbers,' Klavdii said. 'Numbers count for nothing. You cut off the snake's head and the body dies. His soldiers will fall in line, once he's out of the picture,' Laska said. 'What about Alik?' Klavdii asked. 'Alik is a weak druggie. He won't dare challenge me. But I'll kill him anyway, just because I never liked him,' Laska answered.

"And then they laughed like a couple of crazy killers from an eighties horror movie," Raisa concluded.

Kazimir diverts his attention back to Klavdii.

"Boss, please tell me you don't believe that story?" Klavdii asks.

"Yes, I do believe it. Because you see, no one here ever mentioned Alik. How would she even know he exists if not for your conversation with Laska?"

"Maybe she heard the name someplace else," Odin suggests.

"Possible, but she also mentioned Alik's drug problem. Only a few are privy to that information. Klavdii just tell the truth and I promise Odin will not kill you," Kazimir says.

Klavdii looks up at Odin with doubt.

"Put your gun away," Kazimir instructs Odin.

Odin holsters his weapon.

"The truth Klavdii!" Kazimir yells.

"All right boss, she's telling the truth. Laska was planning to usurp control."

Kazimir scoffs.

"And what about Klavdii? Do you wish my demise as well?"

"No boss, but you must understand. I'm a soldier of fortune. I do what I'm told by the highest bidder, no questions asked," Klavdii explains.

"So, you just go with the flow? I understand that. In fact, I'm not even angry with you. And to show my good faith, I'm going to keep my promise. Odin is not going to kill you. Because you were nice enough to tell me the truth; I'm going to kill you myself."

Kazimir draws his gun and shoots Klavdii in the chest. Klavdii slumps over and gasps for air. Jedrek pulls a shocked Raisa closer.

"Get this piece of crap out of my office. You know where to take him. I'll be there to finish him momentarily," Kazimir says putting his gun down.

Two men grab Klavdii and drag him away while he yet clings to life.

"It appears you did me a favor by disposing of my nephew for me," Kazimir says.

"Are you going to let us go?" Raisa asks.

"Unfortunately, I can't let you go," Kazimir responds.

"Why not?" Jedrek asks.

"You've seen and heard too much. I can't afford to let you walk away. No matter how much I like you."

"We won't tell anyone," Raisa says.

"I can't take that chance," Kazimir says.

"After what I did to your nephew. Why would I go blabbing to people about what I saw or heard?" Jedrek asks.

"Laska's body was already cremated. There's virtually no evidence of his existence. After all, we could not have an open casket funeral with what you did to his face," Kazimir says.

"But you said you liked us," Raisa says.

"I do like you. I like you so much, I'm going to spare you the torturous gruesome death I promised your husband. I don't have the heart to kill you myself. My men will carry out the deed. It will be quick and painless. That is how much I like you," Kazimir explains.

"Why?" Raisa questions.

"You must understand, it's no longer personal, it's just business."

Raisa gets down on her knees.

"Begging for mercy won't do you any good," Kazimir says.

Raisa closes her eyes and begins to pray.

"Get up! Meet your fate with dignity," Kazimir commands.

"She's not begging for mercy, she's praying," Jedrek smiles at her.

"Praying to whom?" Kazimir asks.

"To God!" Jedrek says with an angry tone.

"God?" Kazimir asks.

Odin and the other men laugh.

"Where is your God to save you? Why doesn't He ascend from the heavens to protect you? Your prayers are falling on deaf ears. So just stop it girl, you're only embarrassing yourself," Kazimir says.

Jedrek kneels beside Raisa and holds her hand.

"Keep praying baby," Jedrek says closing his eyes.

"Stop that!" Kazimir demands.

"Or what, you'll shoot us?" Jedrek inquires.

"I said, stop it!" Kazimir shouts.

The men look on in amazement as the couple dares to defy Kazimir.

"Get them out of here," Kazimir calmly states.

Odin snatches Jedrek away from Raisa and onto his feet.

"Let's go," the tall man says to Raisa.

She raises her index finger to suggest the man wait a moment.

"Amen," Raisa says.

"Amen," Jedrek concurs.

Jedrek extends his hand to Raisa and helps her up.

"I love you, Jedrek Mann," she says.

"Not as much as I love you, Raisa Mann," he replies.

They smile at each other.

"Boss?" The tall man asks with uncertainty.

"You have your orders, take them," Kazimir says.

Jedrek continues to hold Raisa's hand as they are escorted out. Alik enters the room halting their exit.

"Well, it's about time you showed up," Kazimir says.

I beg your forgiveness father. I had pressing business to attend to," Alik responds.

Alik notices Jedrek and Raisa.

"Hey, I know this man," Alik says.

"You should, he's the one that killed Laska," Kazimir says.

"No, I know him from before. So, you killed Laska? I'm sure you had a good reason; with Laska's track record for offending people," Alik explains.

"Yes, he had good cause, nevertheless they must be disposed of. For I fear they have seen and heard too much about my business," Kazimir says.

"If that's all there is, I can assure you; this man is not a rat," Alik says pointing at Jedrek.

"How do you know?" Kazimir asks.

"This is the guy I told you about. The one from jail," Alik says.

"Refresh my memory," Kazimir says.

"Do you remember a while ago, when you left me in jail; to try to teach me a lesson?" Alik asks.

"It was for your own good. You were using the stuff you were supposed to sell," Kazimir explains.

"It's just as easy to get drugs in jail as it is on the streets. A hard lesson Dimitri learned."

"Get to the point Alik," Kazimir demands."

"We continued using, even in jail. The day Dimitri died; we were supposed to meet up; to share a hit. But he got robbed and killed by another fiend. There was only one witness to the murder. That man was Jedrek. But he refused to talk to the guards about what he saw.

"My Aryan allies and I paid Jedrek a visit. We cornered him; being sure he would tell us who killed Dimitri. Even with being threatened with a beating, he refused to talk. Jedrek wasn't afraid to die. He took all seven of us on as best he could. Jedrek managed to knock a man out cold, broke one man's nose, and busted another man's jaw before we overpowered him.

"We beat him within an inch of life. The Aryans wanted to kill him, but I suggested we use him as bait. Allowing the killer to think we spared Jedrek's life in exchange for information. The trap was set.

Jedrek was taken to the infirmary. That is where the killer would strike. After all, nobody likes a snitch.

"I watched and waited to ambush the killer. It was supposed to be a two-for-one deal. I would let the killer have Jedrek, then I'd claim the killer's life for Dimitri. But sometimes things don't go as we plan," Alik says.

"What happened? The killer didn't show?" Kazimir asks.

"He showed, but what happened next was something like a Greek myth. The man tried to kill Jedrek, but he refused to die. Half dead Jedrek fought for his life. The guy had a shiv and he tried to carve Jedrek like a Thanksgiving turkey. That is how Jedrek got that scar on his face.

"Somehow, Jedrek was able to reverse the blade and stab the man in the throat. The man died almost instantly. It was marvelous. I saw Dimitri avenged. They ruled in favor of Jedrek, stating it was self-defense. I never thanked you Jedrek," Alik says.

"I didn't have a choice. I fought to survive," Jedrek says.

"I know, but nevertheless the deed was done. Therefore, I owe you. I ask that you pardon them father," Alik requests.

"No, the debt was settled when you let him live. I'm not going to honor Jedrek for avenging the death of a known druggie," Kazimir says.

"Dimitri was the closest thing I had to a brother. I honor him by allowing Jedrek his life. If you won't spare Jedrek for Dimitri, then spare him for my life."

"May I remind you; Dimitri was the one that got you hooked in the first place. And you sought to avenge his death like an angry widow," Kazimir says.

Jedrek and Raisa continue to watch as father and son argue over their fate.

"Jedrek never mentioned who put him in the infirmary. He kept his mouth shut about all of it and he never tried to retaliate against me," Alik says.

"He did so, out of fear," Kazimir argues.

"I don't think he was afraid. It was speculated, that Jedrek had God on his side. He was untouchable after that day in the infirmary," Alik says.

"Enough! I'm getting bored of hearing about the legend of Jedrek. You waltz in here and want to stake a claim on his life. You want to spare this man. This is proof you don't have the stomach to be my successor. The past has nothing to do with this. You have nothing to do with this. You were too busy to help us while we were hunting him. So, you don't have a say in the matter now."

"I was busy taking care of a problem."

"What sort of problem was so important you couldn't answer your phone?"

"Officer Arnold called me. Apparently, he got busted by one of his own."

Kazimir laughs.

"There are still some good cops left in Tea Town?" Kazimir asks.

"He called me when he couldn't get ahold of Laska. He knew better than to call you," Alik says.

Kazimir smiles.

"I went to see him; bailed him out. He started complaining about the officer that arrested him and how his career was over with. He said it was our fault because he got caught doing our dirty work. He needed money to disappear; felt we owed it to him. He threatened to talk; said he knew enough to bury us," Alik explains.

"Officer Arnold is a snake," Kazimir says.

"One we no longer had use for. I took care of him," Alik says.

"You, all by yourself?" Kazimir asks.

"Yes," Alik answers.

"I'm curious as to what you did with him afterwards."

"No one will ever know unless Veles speaks of it from the underworld."

Kazimir claps.

"You thought like a true boss, and you didn't mind getting your hands dirty. I respect that. You cleaned your mess like a man. You made progress today but you're still not ready to be the boss. There's so much more I must teach you. Sit down and watch how it's done," Kazimir says.

"No, I won't. In hindsight, Jedrek could have retaliated against me, but he chose not to. I don't think he was held by fear. I think he forgave me. Whatever the reason, he spared my life father. I owe him, a life for a life. You told me we must always repay our debts and our word is our bond."

Kazimir looks at Odin.

"You did say that," Odin reminds him.

"You're using my own words against me. I'm glad to see you were paying attention. I misjudged you. You're one step closer to filling my shoes someday," Kazimir says with pride.

Kazimir reverts his attention to Jedrek and Raisa.

"In honor of my son's request, I grant you life. It looks like your God has answered your prayer," he says holding his thumb up.

"I wasn't praying for my soul, I was praying for yours," Raisa says.

Kazimir is confounded. Jedrek smiles.

"Don't ever let me see your faces again, or the next time I might not be so merciful," Kazimir says.

Jedrek gives Kazimir a death stare. Kazimir and his men laugh.

"I like this guy. He would have made a good soldier," Kazimir says.

"I've paid my debt, now go in peace. But don't mistake me for a friend. If I see you again, I'll treat you like an enemy," Alik warns.

The couple turns to walk out.

"Oh, by the way, you may want to disappear for a while. Some people are angry about not collecting the reward. They would probably kill you just for kicks. Now go, get out of my sight," Kazimir urges.

They make their exit. Once outside, Jedrek closes his eyes.

"Are you all, right?" She asks.

"I'm good, I had to take a moment to thank Him," he answers.

"He is truly worthy to be praised. Thank you, Jesus," she says looking up.

"I still can't believe what just happened," he says.

"Alik probably has no idea why he pressed so hard for our release."

"It's true what they say. God can use anyone to do His work."

Jedrek hugs Raisa tight.

"I'm ok, they didn't hurt me," she says.

She sees tears in his eyes.

"What's wrong Jeed?"

"I can't believe I almost lost you. You mean everything to me."

She wipes the tears from his eyes.

"Please stop, before you make me cry too," she says with a whimper.

"Ok baby."

They look over the shipyard.

"Where do we go from here, and how do we get there?" Jedrek asks.

A speeding car comes to a screeching halt less than 50 yards from them. Rafiq jumps out of the car and rushes over to meet them. He lets out a deep breath.

"I didn't think I'd see y'all again," Rafiq says.

"Neither did we," Jedrek says.

"What happened?" Rafiq asks.

"It's a long story, with several twists and turns. I'll have to tell you some other time. For now, we're just thinking about our next move," Jedrek replies.

"Yeah man, I hear that," Rafiq says glancing at Raisa.

Raisa looks away.

"I'm sorry I shot you," she says.

"Wait? What? You shot him?" Jedrek asks.

"Don't ever feel sorry for shooting me. You did what you had to do for your man. If I were in your shoes, I would've done the same thing. So, no hard feelings."

They fist bump.

"What happened after I left the safe house?" Jedrek asks.

"Hey, it's a long story, with several twists and turns," Rafiq says.

They all laugh.

"I would've been here sooner, but I had to get Burn to the hospital."

"Is he ok?" Jedrek asks.

"Yeah, he's ok, Thank God," Rafiq answers.

"I don't mean to be rude, but we should probably get out of here before someone sees us," Raisa suggests.

Rafiq hands Jedrek the keys.

"Take the car, I'm staying," Rafiq says.

"Why?" They both ask.

"I'm going in there to tell Kazimir I'm done," Rafiq explains.

"You're done, just like that?" Jedrek asks.

"Just like that. You were right about me Jed; you and your wife both. I'm not living a good life. Up until now, I've only existed. These last few days with y'all have made me reexamine things. I have a feeling I haven't had in a long time. A feeling of…"

"Peace?" Raisa asks.

"Yes, peace; I want more of it. I need more of it. There's more to life than hustling in Tea Town. I used to consider myself a success. But I'll gladly trade success for happiness. I wanna realize my true purpose," Rafiq says.

Jedrek nods his head.

"I'm not gonna hold y'all up. Be safe; put some distance between y'all and this city. Whatever you do, don't go back to your house," Rafiq says.

"I'm sure Kazimir's men did a number on it," Jedrek says.

"That's not something you should see right now," Rafiq says.

"Like my shop?" Jedrek asks.

Rafiq hangs his head. Raisa wraps her arms around Jedrek.

"They're only material things," she says.

"You have a good woman, Jed. She's willing to kill for you. If I hadn't been wearing my vest, she probably would've killed me," Rafiq says.

Raisa smirks.

"You sure about going in there alone?" Jedrek asks.

"Most people think Kazimir is scary. You don't wanna know what I would've done to him if he'd hurt you two," Rafiq responds.

"I'm glad it didn't have to come to that."

"I'll be fine. I'm gonna make Kazimir an offer he won't refuse. And the money we discussed; I want you to take half of it," Rafiq says.

"You know I can't take that money Ra."

"Yeah, I know."

"We'll be fine. We have some money saved. It should tide us over for a while. Thanks though; thank you for everything you've done for us," Jedrek says.

No bro, I thank both of you for opening my eyes. You've done all right for yourself. I'm proud of you brother. I love you man," Rafiq says.

"I love you too bro."

"Bye Ra-Ra and thank you for everything," Raisa says.

"Ra-Ra?" Rafiq asks.

"That's something she does. If she's given you a nickname, that means she considers you family," Jedrek explains.

Rafiq smiles.

"You're a true virtuous woman Raisa. I see why Jedrek loves you so much."

"Yeah, with all my heart and soul."

Jedrek leans in to kiss Raisa on her cheek. She turns her head and playfully snaps her teeth at him. They all laugh.

In the months that followed, Raisa and Jedrek sold their house and the shop. They moved to a small town called Polk Field. It's a peaceful slow-paced town; they like it a lot. Raisa reconnected with her family. And just as she thought, they fell in love with Jedrek instantly. Rafiq stayed true to his word and left his criminal life behind. He bought the old studio and along with Burn, launched R&B Records.

Signing their first artist, Raisa Mann to a multi-album recording deal. I hear Raisa will be the opening act for Calena Marie's national tour. Raisa's doctor cleared her to go on tour. He advised her to get plenty of rest during her downtime. You know, with her being pregnant and all. If it's a girl, they plan to name her Alice; in honor of Jedrek's grandmother.

I'd like to tell you that Kazimir turned over a new leaf. Unfortunately, he's still a homicidal madman. Sometime after Jedrek and Raisa left Tea Town, Kazimir's hotel mysteriously burned to the ground. No one was injured but several girls managed to escape. Witnesses reported seeing a tall man wearing a black hoodie fleeing the scene.

"If our lives were a movie, it would have a happy ending," Jedrek says.

The End

Special Thanks To

The Moore Family

Cheryl Cross

Kaitlin Barkley

Suzanne Elliott

Made in the USA
Columbia, SC
11 July 2022

63307311R00153